While the events described and some of the characters in this book may be based on actual historical events and real people, Peter Rogers is a fictional character, created by the author, and his story is a work of fiction.

Scholastic Children's Books
Commonwealth House, 1–19 New Oxford Street,
London, WC1A 1NU, UK
A division of Scholastic Ltd
London ~ New York ~ Toronto ~ Sydney ~ Auckland
Mexico City ~ New Delhi ~ Hong Kong

Published in the UK by Scholastic Ltd, 2005
This edition published 2014

Copyright © Bryan Perrett, 2005

ISBN 978 1407 13674 5

Printed and bound by CPI Group (UK) Ltd, Croydon, CR0 4YY

2 4 6 8 10 9 7 5 3 1

The right of Bryan Perrett to be identified as the author of this work has been asserted by him in accordance with the Copyright, Designs and Patents Act, 1988.

U-BOAT HUNTER

SCHOLASTIC

BRYAN PERRETT

LIVERPOOL, 1939

My name is Peter Rogers and I served as a signalman aboard HMS Arum throughout the Battle of the Atlantic. Our task was to escort the convoys of merchant vessels carrying vital supplies of food and war materials. Without these Great Britain would have been unable to continue fighting and we might have lost the War. It was a battle we won because we had to, although it cost the lives of no less than 30,000 merchant seamen. This is the story of my part in that battle, and of my quest for revenge on one U-boat captain in particular…

I have always been interested in ships and the sea, which is not surprising as I was born and brought up in Liverpool, one of the world's major ports. Every day, ships of all shapes and sizes left the River Mersey bound for foreign parts. There were smart passenger liners and there were freighters carrying every kind of cargo you can think of. And every day more liners and freighters would arrive in the port from every part of the globe. Sometimes I would stand at Pier Head, looking down the river to the open sea and the wide sky at its mouth, knowing that beyond lay all the exciting and strange-sounding places other people talked about. By the time I was ten I had grown determined that one day I, too, would go to sea and visit them all – and return home with my own tales to tell.

My father was skipper of a cargo ship named *Antigua Moon*. Along with a dozen similar freighters, the ship was owned by Moon and Dexter Ltd of Liverpool and traded round the Caribbean and along the east coast of South America. It was easy to identify a Moon Line ship in the Mersey – they had black funnels and the sickle moon in a broad blue band. I had been aboard *Antigua Moon* so many times that I could find my way around her blindfolded. Her officers were regular visitors to our home, and I had played football and cricket with them in the garden so often that they had become like uncles to me. I knew many of the seamen by name as well. Most were British, but there were some West Indians and South Americans as well. I thought that they were all very friendly, but Dad said that they were a wild bunch. They were, however, no match for Roddy Maguire, *Antigua Moon*'s tough boatswain, who was also a regular at my father's house.

My school was the training ship *Conway*. In the nineteenth century she had been a Royal Navy warship and still retained her black-and-white hull and fully rigged masts. Her role now – as well as providing a good general education – was to prepare boys for a career as officers in the merchant navy. Many of those who joined the merchant service also volunteered for the Royal Naval Reserve in time of war. We slept in hammocks between decks, were governed by a strict naval routine and became familiar with the language of the sea. Our nautical classes gave us a good grounding in navigation, signalling with flags and lamps, boat handling, sailing and other subjects. In 1939 *Conway* was moored off Tranmere, on the Cheshire side of the River Mersey. From the ship, I could just about see our house in Cressington, a suburb of Liverpool, across the river – although I lived aboard ship in term time.

On 1 September 1939 Germany invaded Poland. Two days later the United Kingdom declared war on Germany when its government refused to withdraw its troops. The Second World War had therefore started when the autumn term on *Conway* began. The Admiralty had already announced that merchant shipping to and from the United Kingdom would sail in escorted convoys, but this would take time to organize as many individual ships were still making their way home. This worried me, because I knew that *Antigua Moon* was one of them, and the enemy had already started attacking our ships – the passenger liner *Athenia* had been sunk less than 24 hours after the declaration of war.

One morning, towards the end of September, I was working on a problem in navigation class when the Captain's secretary entered the room and whispered something to the instructor. He nodded and looked in my direction.

"Rogers, you can stop what you're doing," he said. "The Captain's got some news for you, so you'd better lay aft right away."

Fearing the worst, I hurried to the Captain's cabin, knocked and was told to enter.

"Don't look so worried, Peter," said the Captain, seeing

my anxious expression. "I've just had a telephone call from your father."

I felt a little better, but as Christian names were only used when someone had personal problems, I knew that there was going to be bad news.

"He's safe and well, but his ship was torpedoed and sunk off the west coast of Ireland a week ago," the Captain continued. "It's not policy to report individual sinkings, and as the survivors have only just reached Liverpool this is the first we've heard of it. I really am very sorry."

Even though I had been half expecting something like this, it was still a terrible shock. I felt the blood drain from my face.

"Survivors?" I heard myself say, almost as though it was someone else speaking. "Does that mean…?"

"Yes, I'm afraid that there was some loss of life," replied the Captain. "Now, I know your father will be glad to see you, Peter, so I'm giving you a few days' leave."

After the Captain dismissed me, I packed my kit and was rowed ashore, little realizing then that I would not be returning to *Conway*. The electric-train journey under the river and the tram ride from Central Station passed in a sort of dream as I tried to accept that a large part of my world had gone for ever.

Dad opened the door, trying to look as cheerful as he always did when I came back from school. I thought he looked older and thinner than when I had last seen him.

"Hello, Dad – I'm glad you're all right," was all I could think of to say.

"Well, we've got Roddy Maguire to thank for that," he replied.

"What happened?" I asked, as I followed him into the house.

"Once I knew that war had broken out, I decided to alter course," he said. "As you know, we usually enter the Irish Sea by St George's Channel, between Ireland and South Wales. During the last war we lost a lot of ships on this approach, including *Lusitania*, and that's where I thought the U-boats – as the Germans call their submarines – might be waiting for us this time, so I decided to skirt the north coast of Ireland and come home through the North Channel instead. It seems that I made a mistake. At about three o'clock in the morning we were off the coast of Donegal when we were hit on the port side by two torpedoes, one forward and one in the boiler room. The boiler-room lads never stood a chance."

He paused, and I knew he was thinking of the horrors that the stokers must have endured – the explosions, the sudden darkness, the immense inrush of water, and the super-heated steam from the ruptured boilers that would have flayed the skin from their bones before they could reach the ladders that would lead them to safety.

"I knew she was lost," he continued, with great sadness in his voice. "She was down by the bows and starting to list to port. I gave the order to abandon ship. Most people got away in two of the port-side boats. After Roddy Maguire and I checked that no one was left alive, the rest of us got away in one of the starboard boats. Now, when a ship goes down, she creates a lot of suction and she'll take a boat down with her if it's too close, so we concentrated on rowing as far away as we could get before she disappeared. That's why I had no idea what was happening on the far side of her."

"What d'you mean?" I asked.

"Well, she took about twenty minutes to die," he replied. "She went with a rush, her stern upended and lying on her side. The sea seemed to boil over her as trapped air and all sorts came to the surface. It was then that Roddy grabbed my arm and pointed. The U-boat had surfaced close to our other boats, which were illuminated by a searchlight on its conning tower. Not knowing what to expect, we began rowing towards them, but we were still outside the searchlight's beam. As we got closer, I could see a machine gun being aimed at our boats. The U-boat Captain came down from the conning tower and was joined by several armed men, who emerged from a hatch on the deck. I can't explain it, but I had a feeling that something dreadful was about to happen. I told the men to stop rowing, and we remained hidden in the darkness. While we drifted, I noticed a coat of arms painted on the side of the conning tower – I couldn't quite make it out, but I do know it included a crowned wolf.

"Anyway, sound carries across water, and I heard the Captain shout to the other boats, 'Come alongside. Your officers will join me here on deck.' Jack Edwards, Dick Armitage, Tony Bland and Hamish MacLeod clambered out of their boats and on to the U-boat. Jack always had a fiendish temper and even from a distance I could see he was spoiling for a fight.

'You've sunk our ship – what more do you want?' he shouted at the German Captain.

'As officers of the merchant marines you will be of great service to your country,' I heard the Captain say. "I cannot permit that. You are now prisoners of the German Navy and will spend the rest of the War in a prison camp.'

'Like hell we will!' Jack bellowed. 'We're merchant seamen and that means we're civilians – I demand that you respect that!'

"The Captain turned to his men and snapped an order. One of the Germans grabbed Jack and tried to drag him towards the hatch. Jack rounded on him and thumped him so hard that he went over the side. The Captain pulled out a pistol and shot Jack dead. Then, without pausing, he shot Dick, Tony and Hamish. For a moment there was a stunned silence, then there were shouts of 'Bloody murderer!' and 'You'll swing for that, you swine!' from the boats. Even the Germans seemed shocked. I could see them looking down at the bodies and then at their

Captain in disbelief. The Captain pointed his pistol at the nearest man in the boats.

'Be silent, or I shall send more of you to join them!' he shouted. He then examined the bodies more closely. 'So! Here we have your First, Second and Third Officers and the Chief Engineer – where is your Captain?'

"There was no reply. It was then that Roddy tossed my cap over the side of the boat. 'For God's sake get your jacket off, Skipper, or he'll do for you as well!' he said. I knew he was right. Fortunately, I had pulled on a jersey, so I looked like one of the crew. I heard the U-boat Captain issue an order and the searchlight began scouring the sea. Suddenly, our boat was flooded with light.

'You there – bring your boat alongside! If your Captain is aboard he is to show himself immediately!'

'The Skipper's dead!' shouted Roddy. 'He was killed when your first torpedo exploded.'

'Ach so! And now he is enjoying a jolly reunion with his old friends in hell!' sneered the German, pointing to the bodies at his feet. I would have killed him with my bare hands if I could have got at him. As we got closer I was able to memorize every detail about him, and I'll do everything I can to see that one day he's punished for what he did. I'll never forget his face – it was long, like a horse's, with a long nose separating protruding eyes that were too close together. Hard to tell his age because of his ginger beard, but I'd say he was still in his early twenties. Anyway, he stood there, hands on hips – the arrogant swine – and gave us what he thought was a pep talk.

'You men are lucky,' he said. 'I have decided to let you go on your way because I have a little job for you. When you arrive home you will warn your people that we intend to starve your little island into submission, just as your Royal Navy's blockade starved Germany during the last war. As you have seen tonight, any pointless resistance will be ruthlessly crushed – remember that!'

"He climbed back into the conning tower, his crew went below and the U-boat submerged. We picked up the bodies when they floated clear, hoisted the sails and late the following afternoon we reached Donegal. The Irish treated us very kindly, gave the lads a decent burial, and took us across the Northern Irish border to Londonderry, where I made a full report to the naval authorities. Then we took the train to Belfast and came home on the ferry."

I was too horrified by the story to speak for a while, but at length I asked Dad what the reaction of the ship's owners had been.

"Oh, I went down to see Mr Moon this morning," he replied, an expression of bitterness creeping over his face. "The old skinflint was more worried about the time it will take the government to pay him compensation for the ship and her cargo than the death of her crew."

That didn't surprise me. I had met Josiah Moon several times and I had never liked him. His suit was always covered with tobacco ash, his teeth were yellow, his breath smelled and he sprayed you with spittle when he talked. When he smiled or laughed, I knew he didn't mean it because his eyes remained expressionless behind his thick glasses.

"I'm to take over *Trinidad Moon* when she comes in," continued Dad. "She's the newest in the fleet, so that's something, I suppose, and Bob Cannon, her skipper, was due to retire anyway."

"What about your old crew?" I asked.

"The company will pay the officers' widows a measly pension, and the men will receive their pay up to the day the ship went down. Unless they get a place aboard another ship they'll have a hard time once that has gone."

"That doesn't seem fair after what they've been through," I said.

"I know, but it's the custom," Dad replied, spreading his hands. "Moon says he can't break the agreement he has with the rest of the ship owners. All my lads had were the clothes they stood up in, but he wasn't going to do a darn thing for them until I said it would look bad for the company if it didn't do something to help. In the end, he shelled out one pound apiece for them to replace things like soap, razors and underclothes that they'd lost – and he did even that with a bad grace. 'You can tell them this came out of my own pocket,' he snapped. 'And if I hear they've been wasting it on drink or pleasure they'll never work for this company again!'"

Dad and I talked a little while longer, then I went up to my room to change out of my uniform. The room was full of reminders of my father's friends. There was the beautifully detailed model of *Antigua Moon* that Hamish MacLeod had made for me in his hours off watch, and presents that the other officers had given me from time to time – a voodoo mask from Haiti, a blowpipe from the Amazonian jungles and a Mexican sombrero. Until now it had been difficult for me to accept that these men were really dead, but now the cold reality of it hit me. A bitter hatred for the U-boat Captain rose up inside me. I also disliked Mr Moon more than I had ever done for his callous attitude to the deaths of those who had helped to make him a millionaire.

By the time I went back downstairs Mother had returned from the shops and was making tea. Dad was on the telephone.

"It's your father's old school friend, Edmund Emerson," said Mother. "He's got some news about the sinking."

I knew that Rear Admiral Sir Edmund Emerson had enjoyed a distinguished career in the Royal Navy and that nowadays he was involved in the shadowy world of naval intelligence.

"Many thanks, Edmund – I feel a little better about things now," I heard Dad say as he rang off.

"We know who the swine is," he commented as he sat down at the table. "Edmund says we'll get him, sooner or later, and that even if he survives the War he'll end up dancing the hornpipe on the end of a rope."

"How did he find him so quickly?" I asked.

"Remember that crowned wolf coat of arms he'd painted on the conning tower? Edmund has a chum at the College of Heralds who traced it to the von Schleigen family. You could say that they were robber barons, living in one of those ruined castles you see on hills overlooking the Rhine. Made their money taking illegal tolls from traffic on the river. When that was stopped they took up banking in Munich. Otto, the present head of the family, is a top Nazi who has direct access to Adolf Hitler at any time. Edmund also spoke to our last naval attaché in Berlin, who told him that Otto's eldest son, Klaus, is in the German Navy and commands a U-boat. Apparently, he's just as dedicated a Nazi as his father. Most senior officers can't stand him, but because he's got so much influence there's nothing they can do about him. Anyway, the whole story will be told on tonight's Nine o'Clock News and is also being broadcast on the BBC's World Service. Hitler won't like that sort of publicity one bit."

The news bulletin contained a full account of the way in which *Antigua Moon* officers had been murdered and even named the U-boat Captain as Lt Commander Klaus von Schleigen. It gave us all some satisfaction that details of the crime had been broadcast all over the world. The next day, however, Sir Edmund called again and I could tell from Dad's tone that he wasn't pleased by what he heard.

"It seems that Doctor Goebbel's propaganda ministry in Berlin have broadcast their own version of the story," he said, his face grim as he put down the phone. "They claim that we're trying to destroy the reputation of an honourable man, who had simply asked our officers on to his deck to ensure that they had sufficient provisions and to indicate the course they should take for the Irish coast. In response, they launched a vicious attack and encouraged our crew to board the U-boat and capture it. They say that von Schleigen had been forced to use his pistol to restore order – that he had no other choice."

"But that's a lie!" I burst out angrily.

"Of course it is," Dad replied, shrugging. "The trouble is, as Edmund says, truth is the first casualty in any war. He also says that the position is complicated because so far, a remarkable number of U-boat captains have behaved decently towards survivors. Some have asked whether the men in the lifeboats have enough food and water, and one even towed our boats towards land until there was danger of the U-boat being intercepted by one of our destroyers. However, that sort of thing isn't expected to last much longer. This is going to be a long, ruthless war and it will have to be fought through to the bitter end."

When I thought about everything that had happened and the fact that Dad would be off to sea again in a week or two, returning to school didn't seem important any more. I wanted to play an active part in the War, partly so that I could exact revenge for the death of my old friends, and partly because if I joined the Royal Navy I could help to provide protection for Dad and the rest of the merchant seamen who would be exposed to constant danger for years to come. My sixteenth birthday was only a week away and if I lied about my age I was sure I would be accepted when I volunteered.

With my mind made up I took a tram into the city and went straight to the Royal Navy's recruiting office. There was a crowd there but eventually I found myself in front of a middle-aged, balding Chief Petty Officer with extremely shrewd eyes.

"How old are you, son?" he asked.

"I'm eighteen – just," I replied.

"So am I," he said, with a smile. "Off you go, and come back in a year or two."

"But I'm good at boat handling, I've been taught navigation and I can signal with flags and lamps," I protested indignantly. "I want to volunteer as a signaller."

"Where did you learn all that then?"

I told him and he thought for a moment before replying.

"I'm going to give you some good advice. Go back to school, finish your studies, then get yourself a Junior Mate's ticket on a merchant ship. If you're lucky, your ship might be taken up from trade as an armed merchant cruiser – then you'll be paid at a far better rate than the Royal Navy can afford and still have all the excitement."

I knew that he was telling me, as kindly as possible, that he wouldn't accept me. But I was determined.

"That isn't how it works," I said obstinately. "I'd have to spend three or four years at sea as a cadet before I'd even be allowed to sit the exam for a Junior Mate's ticket, and by then the War might be over. I want to get into the Royal Navy now!"

"Why? What's your hurry, son?"

I told him about the loss of *Antigua Moon* and the murder of her officers. He nodded in understanding.

"Heard about it on last night's news," he said. "In your position I'd feel the same and I'd want to do something about it too. Tell you what I will do. You come back with a letter of approval from your parents and I'll sign you on as an HO rating – that means Hostilities Only, and you'll be discharged when the War's over. I'll stick my neck out for you and we'll forget about your age."

I thanked him, and he nodded, becoming the strict regular Chief Petty Officer again.

"Now listen," he continued. "Just forget any ideas you've got about flashing signals for ships to form battle lines. You'll be doing six weeks' basic training, then a minimum of nine months at sea before you'll even be considered for a signaller's job. If you're chosen, you'll go on a specialist course ashore. If you fail the course, you'll be back where you started. And one other thing – your father will have told you the sea's a big place. You and this rat of a U-boat captain have as much chance of meeting as two ping-pong balls bouncing round in Lime Street Station. Still interested?"

I nodded determinedly and went home, expecting an argument. It wasn't as bad as I thought. Dad supported me, although he didn't like the idea of me leaving *Conway* and made me promise to come back to the merchant service after the War, but Mum wasn't at all keen to let me go.

"There have always been lads younger than Peter at sea," Dad said to her, "and frankly I'd rather he was in a position to defend himself in some way than aboard a merchant ship."

"I don't see why he can't finish his time on *Conway*," Mum replied. "He's only got two years to go, after all. At least he'll be safe there."

"I don't think any of us will be safe in this war," said Dad, thoughtfully. "Look what Hitler's bombers have done to Warsaw already. They've reduced it to ruins and God knows how many innocent civilians have been killed. In due course, the Luftwaffe will give Liverpool a hammering as well, for the very good reason that it's the country's most important Atlantic port."

At length they agreed, reluctantly, to give me the letter

of consent I needed. When I showed it to the Chief Petty Officer the next morning, he handed it back without a word, then told me to sign a form. After I had done that he shook my hand.

"You are now Ordinary Seaman Peter Rogers, aged eighteen," he said with a grin. "You're in a man's world now, son, and you'll be treated like a man. Now go through that door and the surgeon will check you over. After that, go home and wait for the letter telling you where to report – and good luck!"

A fortnight later a buff envelope arrived. It contained a postal order representing my first day's pay, a warrant for a railway ticket, and orders to report to a Royal Navy basic training establishment at Pwllheli in North Wales. At last I was on my way.

December 1939 – March 1940

I emerged from Pwllheli station in a sea of other new recruits; to find a Petty Officer waiting beside two lorries.

"Right, you jolly sailor men," he bellowed, "pick up your parrots and monkeys, and get aboard those trucks – lively now if you want any tea!"

The lorries took us to a requisitioned holiday camp, but the next six weeks were anything but a holiday and could hardly be described as jolly. We were taught how to dress properly in naval rig and were drilled endlessly on the parade ground, with and without arms, and we learned how to fire a rifle. We also learned the language of the sea and how to look after ourselves when afloat. I had a slight advantage here as most of my companions had no idea how to sling a hammock, let alone stay in it. There was also some boat work, in which I felt quite at home. At the end of that period we were sent to a holding barracks in Portsmouth to await postings to our ships or overseas. For me, this was a very boring period as it involved handling large quantities of ships' stores, but at least I managed to get home on Christmas leave.

The orders that I received in the new year said that I was to join HMS *Arum*, which was making ready for sea at Smith's Dock, South Shields. I had no idea what kind of warship she was but I hoped she was one of the lean, fast destroyers that always seemed to be in action. After a long train journey, I reached South Shields and made my way to Smith's Dock. There were several ships under construction, but only one was in a finished state. At first glance I was sure that she couldn't be *Arum*, although there were no other warships lying out in the Tyne. On the Mersey we had two big, powerful ocean-going tugs, *Nelson* and *Rodney*. She wasn't much larger than them, although she did mount a gun forward. Was she, I wondered, some sort of armed tug? Was I really going to spend the War aboard such a ship? As I walked alongside her I noticed a Chief Petty Officer and a seaman watching from the head of the gangway.

"You lost, sailor?" barked the CPO.

"Yes, Chief – I'm looking for *Arum*."

"You've found her. Come aboard."

Although in the years ahead I would come to love little *Arum*, at the moment I was bitterly disappointed. I mounted the gangway, saluted the quarterdeck as I had been taught, and handed over my documents.

"Just out of training, I see," noted the CPO, glancing through the papers. "Good report, too. All right, Smudger, take him below and tell Slim to show him the ropes."

"Right, this way, lad," said Smudger. He led me down a companionway to the mess deck and shouted for Slim. When he appeared, Able Seaman Stan Morris was anything but slim. He weighed about 15 stone, had unruly fair hair and a permanent good-humoured grin that exposed the gap between his front teeth. He wore the badge of a signaller on his sleeve.

"This is Ordinary Seaman Rogers," said Smudger. "Just out of training. Chief says you're his sea daddy."

"OK by me, Smudge," said Slim. "Come on, I'll show you where to stow your gear."

"What does he mean – sea daddy?" I asked as Smudger made his way back on deck.

"Means I show you round the ship," replied Slim with a cackling sort of laugh. "Explain the routine, stop you getting yourself into trouble for the first few days."

"She's very small, isn't she?" I said, glancing round the cramped mess deck.

"After five years in the Navy I can tell you that small ships are best," replied Slim. "On big ships like the battle wagons and the cruisers, it's all polishing brass, scrubbing decks and strict routine. On little ships you still do the job they pay you for, but you get to know everyone and it's more matey."

After I had stowed my gear, Slim took me back on deck, where working parties were bringing stores aboard from lorries parked on the quayside.

"Best make your number with Jimmy first, or you'll cop it," he said.

I thought I knew sea talk, but it seemed that the Navy had a language all its own, and I asked him what he meant.

"You report to Jimmy the One – that is, the First Lieutenant – when you join a ship. Ours is Mr Rooney. He's responsible for discipline, arranging the watches, damage-control parties and the like."

We found Lieutenant Rooney in the tiny ship's office, going through papers with the clerk, who I learned was called a Writer. He was clearly harassed and trying to do half a dozen things at once.

"Ordinary Seaman Rogers reporting, sir," I said, saluting.

"What? Oh, yes," responded Mr Rooney, glancing up briefly. He consulted a clipboard, told me that I belonged to the Starboard Watch, where my action station was, and which damage-control party I was to join if the need arose.

"You his sea daddy, Mason?" he asked, turning to Slim.

"Yes, sir."

"Good. Make sure he knows where to go and what to do when he gets there."

"Aye aye, sir."

As we left the office I heard raised voices and glanced up to the open bridge, where a tall, dark officer was arguing fiercely with a man in a bowler hat.

"That's the skipper, Lieutenant Commander Kemp," said

Slim. "As far as we're concerned, he's one of God's relations, so stay out of his way and don't speak to him unless he speaks to you. Looks like he's giving one of the dockyard foremen a hard time."

Below the bridge lay the wheelhouse and chart room. Through a window I could see another officer sorting through piles of charts.

"Mr Swinson, the Navigating Officer," said Slim, then pointed to an officer superintending a group of men working around the gun. "And that's Mr Rutherford, the Gunnery Officer, checking over the 4-inch with his crew."

As we began walking back towards the stern, I asked him whether the 4-inch gun was our only armament.

"No, we've got a couple of Lewis machine guns for use against aircraft," he replied. "They date from the last war, like the 4-inch, and we're all hoping for something better before too long."

He pointed to two racks, each holding nine drums, at the stern. Nearby were two more drums, mounted on top of what looked like mortars.

"These are our depth-charge racks and throwers," he said. "We carry fifty depth charges. Once we've located a U-boat, we steam over her and roll 'em out of the racks over the stern while the throwers fling one out on either side – the idea being that the combined explosions crack open the submarine's hull. We're not as harmless as we look."

Lorries were still delivering stores on the quay, where they were being checked against a list by a young Sub-Lieutenant.

"That's Mr Merredew," said Slim. "His dad's the Commodore of a posh yacht club on the Isle of Wight. Forced him into the Royal Naval Volunteer Reserve by all accounts. Pity, because he's not got much idea what he's doing and no confidence in himself. The other officers give him a hard time. If he doesn't shape up they'll get rid of him."

Along the deck, a grey-haired man of about 40 emerged from the engine room. He leaned on the rail and puffed his pipe contentedly as he watched the traffic on the river. I could see an Engineering Lieutenant's rings on the shoulder straps of his overalls.

"Now there's a happy man," said Slim. "That's our Chief Engineer, Mr Parry. Came in over the bows – that is, worked his way up through the ranks to get his commission. Couldn't care less what goes on up here as long as his machinery ticks over nicely."

"What kind of ship is this?" I asked, feeling terribly ignorant. "At first I thought she was an armed tug, or maybe a minesweeper, but she isn't equipped with the gear for either."

"Ha! Ha! You're right there, matey!" replied Slim, giving one of his cackles. "We're one of the first of a new type of warship called corvettes. We belong to the Flower Class. Early last year someone with brains at the Admiralty saw war coming and realized that we were short of long-range convoy escorts. They wanted something simple that could be built quickly in small yards like this one. In the end they decided to adapt the design of a whaler – and a nice little job they've made of it, too. We've only got one propeller, but that will shove us along at speeds of up to 16 knots, which is enough for U-boat hunting, and at 12 knots we can steam for over 3,400 miles. Mind you, she rolls badly – some say she'd roll on wet grass, given the chance. Anyway, come and meet the most important man on the ship."

We followed a delicious smell to the small galley, where a tall, thin cook was preparing dinner.

"This is Chalky White," said Slim. "What's for scoff, mate? Smells good."

"You'll find out soon enough, you fat lump!" responded Chalky. "Eats enough for half his watch, he does – don't know where they find uniforms big enough for him! Here – saved you a couple of snorkers from breakfast. Now, stop bothering me."

Next, Slim showed me my action station, which was by the depth-charge racks, and where my damage-control party would assemble. He told me that these were just temporary assignments that would change once we were at sea and the officers had a chance to size everyone up. Just as he finished explaining this to me the ship's tannoy loudspeakers crackled into life.

"D'ye hear there! Hands to dinner!"

Back down on the mess deck Chalky was dishing out food to a line of ratings.

"C'mon, me lucky lads – it's Snake and Pigmy followed by Chinese Wedding Cake and Char!"

"What he means is steak and kidney pie followed by rice pudding with raisins and tea," said Slim.

The food was extremely good and during the meal I met some of the others on my watch. Everyone had a nickname that was used instead of their real name. Smudger's was obviously Smith, like all the Smudgers I had ever met. Likewise, I could understand the reasons for Slim and Chalky, and Sparks, too, – the name given to telegraphist Johnny Haworth, a radio operator. However, I couldn't work out why the big, cheerful, well-built man sitting next to me was called Cabby when his real name was Jack Pearson. It couldn't be anything to do with his work on board because he was the gun-layer on the 4-inch. He told me it was because he had once been a London taxi driver. Sometimes he used Cockney rhyming slang, saying "dog and bone" when he meant telephone. Because I was the youngest and smallest aboard, I was promptly named Nipper. The nickname stayed with me throughout my five years aboard *Arum*, despite the fact that during that time I grew a lot and actually became taller than some of the other men.

"What have they got you down for, Nipper?" asked Slim.

"I'm hoping to be a signaller, like you," I replied.

"They call us bunting tossers," he replied, grinning his toothy grin. "Can you do semaphore or Morse?"

"I've done a bit of both, but I'm not very fast."

"OK. Just watch my eye – I'm going to send you a message."

He began a series of long and short winks that I recognized as Morse, but they were too quick for me to pick up all the words.

"Now then, what did I say?" he asked.

"I'm not sure. I got a few of the letters but you were sending too fast for me."

He repeated the message, more slowly.

"You said, 'Pass the salt please,'" I said, "so here it is."

Everyone laughed at that and I began to feel at home.

"Well done," said Slim. "You'll have to increase your speed a bit, but everyone's got to start somewhere."

We talked about the War for a while. The fighting in Poland had ended in a German victory, but in France, where the British Expeditionary Force held part of the line alongside the French Army, there was no fighting at all. This seemed rather odd to us, as the war at sea was being fought without let-up. During its first weeks, a U-boat had penetrated the Home Fleet's apparently safe anchorage at Scapa Flow, sunk the battleship Royal Oak and made good its escape.

"Cheeky blighter!" exclaimed Cabby. "If he wasn't a Jerry, you'd say he deserved to get away with it!"

"Yes, but we got our own back at the Battle of the River Plate, didn't we?" Sparks replied. "Three of our cruisers, *Ajax*, *Achilles* and *Exeter*, had a run-in with Hitler's favourite pocket battleship, *Graf Spee*, remember? She could have swatted any one of them, but they gave her what for and she ran for it. Ended up scuttling herself, didn't she?"

There was a murmur of approval round the table. From my point of view, however, the news wasn't all good. The government had decided to arm merchant ships as a defence against surface attacks by U-boats and commerce raiders. The armament consisted of a single old gun mounted on the stern to show that it was for defensive purposes only. Hitler had responded by announcing that any ship so armed would be treated as a warship and sunk on sight. My thoughts turned to Dad, who was now back at sea with his new command, and I wondered what he made of it all. Ships were now sailing in escorted convoys, although the escorts were few and the number of merchant vessels lost was rising steadily. It was true that we had begun to sink U-boats, but the Germans had started a huge programme of U-boat construction and had plenty of replacements for their lost submarines. It was very worrying.

After dinner we worked for an hour or two, stowing ammunition and stores, then turned in. I had just begun to drop off when I realized that someone was slinging his hammock next to mine.

"How do? I'm Pete Thomas," he said. "Didn't think I'd get here, the trains are in such a state. Jerry's bombed a junction in the Midlands, so mine was re-routed and I've been taken all over the place."

I asked him what his job aboard was and he said that he was an Asdic operator.

"What's Asdic?" I asked.

"It stands for Anti-Submarine Detection Investigation Committee," he replied. "We're fitted with a transmitter that sends out a sound signal through the water ahead of the ship. It sounds like this: ping ... ping ... ping ... ping. Now when it hits something, like a submarine, it bounces back and sounds like this: ping ... ga."

"What do you do then?"

"Well, we know how far away we are from the target because of the time the echo takes to come back, and we know which direction it's coming from, so we chase it. As we get closer the time between the ping and the echo gets shorter. When we're over the target we get a simultaneous echo – pingga!"

"What happens next?" I asked, fascinated.

"I'll ping the side of his head if he doesn't pipe down and let us get some sleep!" shouted Cabby from down the line of hammocks. "That's what'll happen next!"

"That's when we let go of our depth charges," whispered Pete, tapping the side of his nose as though he was letting me into some dark secret. I drifted off to sleep, thinking about how exciting it would be to go chasing after those U-boats.

Next morning we put to sea. At last, I thought, I'm off to war – but there were no cheering crowds to see us off, just a couple of dockyard hands who gave us a wave as we moved out into the river. *Arum* began to roll at once, but it wasn't half as bad as when we reached the open sea, where she pitched violently every time she put her bows into a wave. Within an hour, half the ship's company were hanging over the rail being violently sick.

Grinning broadly, the CPO I had met when I came aboard walked past the line of green-faced, miserable men.

"Bit lively for you is it?" he teased. "You'll get used to it. What you need is some work to take your mind off your troubles!"

His name was Clarke. He was firm but fair, and he knew how to get the best out of a crew. For the next few days the Petty Officers drove us without mercy, practising all sorts of drills. Working in teams, we put out imaginary fires and learned how to shore up bulkheads, plug holes in the hull and evacuate casualties from difficult places, as well as carrying out our usual duties. We were also sent to Action Stations regularly until the First Lieutenant was satisfied with our performance. It was just what we needed to occupy the time until everyone found their sea legs. Working in watches of four hours on and four hours off, I learned the value of sleeping whenever I could.

In what I thought was bitterly cold weather – although it wasn't long before I experienced far worse – we sailed round the north coast of Scotland and anchored off Tobermory, a town on the island of Mull. Here, several senior officers came aboard to put us through our paces. With one of our own submarines playing the part of a U-boat, we made a series of dummy attacks. During these, Pete – now known to everyone as Pingy – proved himself to be a very capable Asdic operator and we earned high marks. The 4-inch gun crew also fired five rounds at a screen target towed behind a tug, but only scored hits with the last two.

"Trouble is, the way we roll, we haven't got a steady gun platform," complained Cabby. "The trick is to pick the right moment before we let fly, and I think I've got the hang of it now."

Other exercises included the rescue of survivors, represented by dummies. For this we used the ship's boats or lowered a scramble net over the side. In the latter case, we were told that some survivors might have used the last of their strength to reach the net and would be too exhausted to climb it – they would require assistance. A few of us volunteered to climb down the net and help, and got thoroughly soaked for our trouble.

On such a small ship gossip spread quickly. One day we were discussing Sub-Lieutenant Merredew over dinner; the general opinion was that he wasn't doing at all well.

"He tries too hard," said Slim. "Wants to get things done in a hurry to save himself a roasting. He's inexperienced so he gets himself in a muddle and gives his commands in the wrong order. So far, the Petty Officers have managed to cover up for him, but it can't last."

"You have to feel sorry for the lad," added Sparks. "As if he hasn't got troubles enough – his first name is Scipio!"

"Scipio? You're having us on! What kind of a name is that to give anyone?" asked Cabby, a note of disbelief in his voice.

"His old man's keen on the Roman Army," Sparks replied. "Scipio was a Roman General."

"Don't like the sound of his old man," said Slim. "Seems a bit of a bully. No wonder the lad's not sure of himself."

I saw what they meant a couple of days later. We had been declared operational and were on our way to the Firth of Clyde, off the west coast of Scotland, where a convoy was forming. Around noon I was doing some work up on the bridge when I saw Mr Merredew taking a sighting with his sextant – a navigational instrument used to measure the angle between the sun and the horizon – on the deck below. I expect he wanted to appear keen, as a minute or so later he appeared on the bridge and took another sighting.

"Very commendable, Mr Merredew," commented the

Captain. "Perhaps you'd be kind enough to tell me where we are."

Mr Merredew went below to the chart house and returned with his calculations of longitude and latitude.

"I see – somehow you seem to have placed us inside Belfast town hall," commented the Captain, peering closely at the measurements. "I think you'd better try again."

Mr Merredew tried again – three times – but his results grew more inaccurate every time. As he was sent below once again, I heard the Captain pass a comment to Mr Rooney in a low tone.

"If he can't navigate, Number One, there's no point in his being here. Unless he improves quickly I think we'd better send him ashore while we've got the chance. He can man a desk somewhere."

I felt really sorry for Mr Merredew. My work was finished, so I went down into the chart room, where I found him frantically going through his figures, surrounded by books of tables and sheets of calculations.

"Can I help, sir?" I asked.

"What? Well, maybe," he replied, his eyes darting wildly across the papers spread in front of him. "Don't suppose you know anything about spherical trigonometry, do you?"

I told him that I did. It was like ordinary trigonometry but it allowed for the curvature of the Earth's surface, and the books of tables helped you fix where you were after you had taken a sighting with the sextant at a specific time. I suspected that Mr Merredew knew the theory, but was in too much of a hurry and was too disorganized to apply it properly.

"I saw you take two sightings, sir – one from the deck and the other from the bridge. It's best to stick with one when you're doing your calculations. Then make sure that you use the correct column in the tables, and also that you don't subtract when you should be adding. It's easy if you take things slowly and in the right order."

We bent over the chart and I worked out the position in which he had taken his readings, then said that we should add dead reckoning to get our present position. This meant allowing for the distance we had travelled since, plus any chances of course, wind and tidal flows. Fortunately, the calculation was easy as we had been travelling in a straight line. He agreed and noted it.

"And where did you learn to navigate, Rogers?" said a voice behind me.

It was the Captain. We had been so busy with our work that neither of us were aware that he had come down from the bridge or had any idea of how long he had been standing there.

I explained my background and he asked me to wait for him on the bridge.

"Rogers, report that vessel over there," he snapped

when he returned from the chart room a few minutes later, pointing at a fishing vessel some way off our port bow.

"Trawler, bearing Red Two, range two thousand, proceeding north, speed ten knots, sir."

Red always meant the port or left side of one's own ship, looking forward, and green meant the starboard or right side. The figures that followed indicated the bearing of the other ship in degrees, its distance and speed being estimated.

"Good. Now tell me what's going on at Green four-five," he said, pointing to a distant smudge of smoke to the west.

I peered through the lookout's binoculars. A small coaster appeared in the lens. It was the type Dad called a Clyde Puffer and was obviously on its rounds of the western islands, delivering and picking up cargoes.

"Small cargo vessel, range six miles, proceeding west-by-north, speed six to eight knots, sir."

The Captain nodded, joined the First Lieutenant for a moment, then went below. Mr Rooney turned to me.

"Rogers, I'm reassigning you as bridge lookout," he said. "The Captain thinks you'll be more use to us there. See that you are."

"Aye aye, sir," I replied, feeling as though I had won some sort of prize. Slim, who had been tidying the flag locker, gave me a toothy grin and winked.

Later in the day I was stopped by Mr Merredew.

"I – I'm very grateful to you, Rogers," he stammered. "If

you hadn't t-turned up I think I'd have been sent ashore. As it is, the Captain's g-giving me another chance and I'm going to t-take your advice."

"Best of luck, sir," was all I could think of to say.

During the next few months we noticed that whoever was Officer of the Watch frequently sent Mr Merredew to verify our position, no doubt acting on instructions from the Captain. As I had suggested, Mr Merredew took time over his calculations and began to produce accurate results regularly.

In the Clyde we refuelled, took on extra ammunition and stores, then joined the convoy that was assembling in the Firth. It consisted of ships of all shapes and sizes – freighters large and small, tankers, bulk grain carriers, and an assortment of battered tramp steamers – escorted by two destroyers and ourselves. Two days later the convoy weighed anchor and began moving towards the open sea. Soon, I knew, we would encounter our enemies, the U-boats. I fervently hoped that one of them would be von Schleigen's, and that we would have the chance to send him to a well-deserved early grave, at the bottom of the ocean.

The convoy consisted of 38 ships. It was marshalled in long lines and covered many square miles of sea. Naturally, it travelled at the speed of the slowest ship, which was about seven knots, and this must have been frustrating for those aboard vessels that could go considerably faster. We spent much of our time chasing up stragglers and signalling ships to keep better station. It was immediately apparent that the merchant navy captains, used to being masters of their own world, did not take kindly to being ordered about by us and were sometimes slow to conform.

Dad had told me about the North Atlantic. For the moment, it was just as he described it – a vast, watery desert of grey, tossing waves, but in the years to come I would see it in its many moods and come to respect and fear it. Sometimes, in summer, it would lie in an almost flat calm, and it was then that the convoys were most at risk from U-boats. Then, such rest as we got between watches was regularly disturbed by the Action Stations klaxon. At other times, there would be such huge swells that *Arum* would seem to be climbing a hill then rushing down the other side. I found this worrying at first, but Slim said that she was like a celluloid duck and would float over anything. In contrast, the merchant ships and larger escorts would put their bows into the swell and then seem to shake off the tons of water that crashed on to their forecastles. Full-blown gales were another matter, and they terrified me until I grew used to them. Lines of waves, many feet high with deep troughs between them, were driven by a demonic wind that blew their tops into tatters of flying spray that filled the air, drenching those of us on the open bridge. It was impossible to rest off watch. There was the boom as each wave struck the bow, the clatter as every unsecured item careered about the mess deck as though it had a life of its own, and the horrible up-down, side-to-side corkscrew motion. To venture on to the open deck was suicidal unless lifelines had been rigged – and even then it was extremely dangerous. Worse still, until the gales abated, the galley was unable to provide hot food or drink because of the risk to the cooks of serious burns or scalds.

Just as frightening in their way were fogs, blizzards and continuous rain. It was not just that U-boats found it easy to stalk a convoy and pick off a victim or two in these conditions, there was also the danger that, having lost all but a few yards' visibility, ships would run each other down. Their captains, aware of the risk, would open the distance between one another. By the time the weather cleared the convoy could be scattered across a wide area and it took time to round them all up.

Sometimes, a convoy would be routed round the north of Iceland. In summer there was little darkness, and in winter there was little daylight. I learned what cold really felt like during my first sub-Arctic winter. I wore every stitch I possessed, yet as I peered out from the open bridge my teeth chattered so badly that I could hardly speak. If the weather was rough, spray would seem to freeze in mid-air, leaving my face red-raw and painful after a while. It didn't seem so bad when steaming mugs of kye reached the bridge at regular intervals. Kye was very thick, hot, sweet cocoa and it seemed to warm you from the inside out. At first, I was classed as too young to receive a rum issue, but somehow, thanks to the generosity of my friends, my kye was always well laced with it, and that helped to keep out the cold as well.

All of this lay in the future, though, and for the moment this first trip was full of interest – that is, until we passed through a belt of bad weather three days after leaving the Clyde. Most of us were cold, wet, miserable, deadly tired, unsettled by the ship's constant motion, and very irritable. One night I had just come off watch, soaked to the skin because of rain squalls, and was enjoying a mug of hot tea when the ship made a violent change of course, putting us beam-on to a heavy swell. She rolled horribly. Lockers burst open and everything that was loose was flung about the mess deck. Cabby lost his balance and crashed into me. We both stumbled over a bench and landed on the deck, with him uppermost. I struck my head and must have passed out, because the next thing I remember is being hauled to my feet and half carried to the sick berth. I had a cut on the back of my head which was inspected and bandaged; I was given an aspirin for my cracking headache, and told to sit still for a while. I returned to the mess deck to find everyone clearing up. Most people had sustained cuts and bruises.

"You all right, Nipper?" asked Cabby, who was tidying his locker. He took out a bar of chocolate, broke it and handed me half. "Here, this should put you back on your feet."

I thanked him and picked up several envelopes that had fallen out of the locker. They had a number of strange stamps attached to them. I collected stamps and knew from my catalogues that they were very rare.

"These are worth a fortune," I said, handing them back.

"Bit of an investment, like," he replied. "Bought 'em when I sold the old cab. Don't trust banks and they're safer than cash when you're on the move. Best you keep quiet about 'em, Nipper – don't want to put temptation in anyone's way, do we?"

I was puzzled. I knew that only rich men could afford to buy stamps like these. They would have cost Cabby far more than he would have got for an old taxi. I didn't press him any further, but I began to wonder how he could have got hold of so much money.

At that moment CPO Clarke came down from the bridge. Someone asked him the reason for the violent change of course.

"There was a damn great bulk carrier, right out of his proper station, bearing down on us through the squall. Mr Merredew was the only one to spot it and he gave the orders on his own initiative. If he hadn't, we'd have been cut in two. As it was, we just scraped clear."

There was a moment's thoughtful silence, broken by Slim.

"Looks as though the lad's beginning to shape up."

"And that's what you lot want to do!" snapped the CPO. "Get your gear stowed securely so that next time we have a bit of excitement it doesn't go flying all over the place!"

The next day I had my first sight of the enemy. A big, four-engined aircraft began circling the convoy just outside the range of the destroyers' anti-aircraft guns. Through binoculars I could see the black cross on the side of its fuselage.

"Focke-Wulf Fw 200 Condor," commented Mr Rutherford, the Officer of the Watch. "Developed pre-war as an airliner, now used as a long-range maritime reconnaissance aircraft. Bristles with machine guns and carries a fair bomb-load too. Seems more interested in shadowing us than attacking. My guess is that he's reporting our position back to base. Then the nearest U-boats will be told to intercept us."

The Captain appeared on the bridge, watched the Condor for several minutes, then turned to Slim.

"Make to German aircraft: FOR GOD'S SAKE FLY ROUND THE OTHER WAY. YOU ARE MAKING ME DIZZY."

"Aye aye, sir," said Slim. He manned the big signal lamp and began flashing the message. To my surprise, a light began winking in the cockpit of the aircraft.

"German aircraft replying, sir: ANYTHING TO OBLIGE, OLD BOY," read Slim.

"Hm, chap's got a sense of humour," commented the Captain. "Just the same, I think we can expect trouble shortly."

It came late that afternoon. We were in our usual position, astern of the convoy – one of our jobs being to pick up survivors from any ship that was torpedoed, when suddenly I saw two white streaks in the water, heading for the point we would reach if we continued on our present course.

"Torpedoes running to port!" I yelled at the top of my voice. The Action Stations klaxon began to blare.

"Hard a'port!" shouted the Captain down the helmsman's voice pipe.

"Wheel's hard a'port, sir!" came the answer.

I watched in terrified fascination as the two streaks sped towards us from the left. The ship's bows were coming round towards them, reducing the area exposed to danger.

One of the torpedoes was going to pass ahead of us, but the second would clearly hit us forward of the 4-inch gun mounting. I expected to be blown to kingdom come in a matter of seconds.

"Get down!" I heard someone shouting.

I threw myself to the floor and waited for the impact. Nothing happened. When we stood up I could see that the torpedo had passed under us and was speeding away into the distance.

"Lucky for us there's less water below our bows than there is midships or aft," commented the Captain. "Midships!" he ordered.

We were now heading back along the fast-disappearing torpedo tracks and it was obvious that he was about to launch a counter-attack.

"Stand by to depth charge!" the Captain barked.

The steady ping of the Asdic had become so much a part of our daily lives that we no longer noticed it. For the first time, now, I realized that its rhythm was broken by an echo.

"Target, 2,000 yards, moving left, sir!" came Pingy's voice over the loudspeaker.

The Captain ordered the helmsman to come to port.

"Target still moving left, sir – 1,800 yards!"

We conformed and the Asdic echo became more rapid.

"Midships!"

"Target dead ahead, sir, 1,200 yards!"

The range closed steadily. Ping...ga, ping..ga, ping.ga pingga went the Asdic.

"Simultaneous echo, sir!" said Pingy's voice in the loudspeaker.

"Fire!" shouted the Captain to the depth-charge party.

I heard the mortars cough and saw the drums rolling off their racks over the stern. It seemed like ages before they exploded, far below us. Huge gouts of water erupted and fell back into the sea.

"Hard a'starboard!" ordered the Captain. "We're going to give him a second helping," he added as we came round.

The Asdic had now returned to its regular rhythm. As we reversed course I could see that the area we had depth-charged was recovering from the immense disturbance. A large number of dead fish were floating on the surface of the water. Suddenly a series of large oily bubbles appeared, followed by other objects I could not identify.

"Disturbance ahead, sir!" I reported.

The Captain ordered Slow Ahead and the beat of the engine died away. Slowly we moved through an area now covered in oil, pieces of wood and various items of clothing. For a moment I felt triumphant revenge and hoped that the U-boat was the one whose Captain had murdered our friends. Then Slim made me think again.

"Helluva way to go," he said. "Trapped in an iron coffin hundreds of feet down, then your hull's cracked open by depth charges and icy water rushes in. Don't stand a chance, do you?"

I shuddered at the thought. The Germans were the enemy and it was my duty to fight them, but my personal feud was with von Schleigen, not the entire German Navy. My elation was further deflated by an exchange between the Captain and the First Lieutenant.

"Shall I log a kill, sir?" asked Mr Rooney.

"No, Number One, just log what you see," answered the Captain. "He may be playing an old trick on us – go deep, lie doggo, release some fuel oil and shoot out rubbish through the torpedo tubes to make us think he's a goner. If he was, I'd have expected some sort of human remains to have surfaced by now. My guess is that he's still down there – damaged, perhaps, but still a menace."

For an hour we carried out a thorough search pattern around the area, but the Asdic failed to produce an echo. At last, deciding that even if we hadn't sunk the U-boat at least we had done our job and protected the merchant ships, we hurried after the convoy, which had by now disappeared over the horizon. The next day, however, a medium-sized freighter was torpedoed. She went down quite slowly, so we were able to rescue her survivors from their boats. Until we were able to transfer them to larger vessels, we were horribly crowded below decks. At various times Asdic contacts were made by ourselves and the two destroyers. We all made individual depth-charge attacks, without result. The Captain was furious.

"Once we get a contact the entire escort should hunt it down until it's destroyed!" he commented to Mr Rooney. "As it is, we all mind our own business unless we're directly involved!"

It sounded very sensible to me.

A few days later, heavy smoke appeared on the western horizon. It was the east-bound convoy we were to escort to home waters and was accompanied by a fast liner that had been armed with guns and converted to the role of Armed Merchant Cruiser. We handed over our convoy to the AMC, which would protect it until, in turn, units of the small but growing Royal Canadian Navy would escort it into North American waters.

We had been heading east for several days when one of the smaller freighters broke down. She was Panamanian registered and a terrible rust-bucket that should have gone to the breaker's yard long since. When she failed to appear we were sent back to look for her, but all we found was floating wreckage and half a charred lifeboat that had been blown apart when the torpedo exploded.

The BBC kept us informed of the War's progress elsewhere. The Germans had invaded Denmark and Norway, but while their troops had overrun those countries with ease, at sea the German Navy had not done so well. It was true that we had lost an aircraft carrier and some destroyers, but an impressive number of their heavy and light cruisers had been sunk or seriously damaged, and during two battles at Narvik in Norway we had sunk no less than ten destroyers. The officers' opinion was that the enemy would be unable to fight a surface engagement for some time to come, although the danger from raiders and U-boats still existed.

We took the convoy into Liverpool. It was good to see the Liver Buildings in the distance again, but there was no chance of my getting home. Indeed, once we had done the essential tasks of refuelling and replenishing stores and ammunition, all we wanted to do was sling our hammocks and sleep. For 24 hours, the ship was an oasis of calm.

Our second trip was similar to the first, although the weather was better. There were more Asdic contacts and we expended a lot of depth charges, which at least kept the enemy down and stopped the majority of attacks. Even so, we lost two ships on the way out and one on the way back. That was depressing, but not so depressing as the news from home. In May the Germans launched major offensives in France, Belgium and Holland. Day after day the news grew worse. The Dutch surrendered; the German panzer divisions reached the Channel, cutting the Allied armies in two; the Belgians surrendered; the British Expeditionary Force and some French troops were surrounded at Dunkirk and a major operation was in progress to evacuate them in June. What remained of the French Army was forced to request an armistice, which left the entire west coast of France in enemy hands; and finally, Italy declared war on us, which meant the conflict had now spread to the Mediterranean as well. We were digesting this last piece of news when the mess-deck tannoy speaker crackled.

"D'ye hear there! This is the Captain speaking. You all know what has happened and it is far from pleasant. Despite the loss of more destroyers than we can afford, we can all take pride in the fact that the Navy, assisted by many civilians in craft as small as cabin cruisers, evacuated so many of our troops from Dunkirk. We must, however, accept that we have experienced a major defeat, that the Army has lost most of its tanks, guns and heavy weapons, and that there is a real risk that Britain will be invaded."

He paused to let this sink in. I could almost feel the silence.

"We are now on our own. But we were also alone when the King of Spain sent his Armada against us, and when Napoleon occupied all of Europe. It didn't do them any good and it won't do Hitler any good, either. Nevertheless, our country depends on the Royal Navy for its survival, and our task will be a difficult one. Because the enemy now controls the French and Norwegian ports, he can send his U-boats much further out into the Atlantic. At the same time, most of the bigger convoy escorts will be retained in home waters until the threat of invasion passes. That means that little ships like ours will be doing twice the work with half the resources. It won't be easy, but I know you won't let me or the ship down. That is all."

The tannoy clicked and we sat without speaking, each of us wrapped in our own thoughts.

The rest of our trip was uneventful, and on the return journey we were ordered into a shipyard on the Clyde. There, dockyard workers swarmed aboard, hammering, riveting and welding as they constructed a sort of bandstand aft of the funnel. This was the mounting for quadruple .5-inch Vickers anti-aircraft guns, which considerably increased our defence against air attack. The wardroom steward told us that Mr Merredew had been given the job of Air Defence Officer, largely because none of the other officers wanted it. That might have been true, but he buckled to, studied the manuals and trained his gun crew thoroughly. We also received a number of Lanchester sub-machine guns – which we were told would be used by boarding parties – and were instructed in their use.

The size of the ship's company was increased, too, which meant that life would be a little easier when we were at sea. Cabby and I were walking past the new anti-aircraft mounting when we were hailed by the cockney accent of one of the new arrivals.

"Gawd, if it isn't old Jack Pearson, large as life!"

Cabby started as though he'd been shot. The man – short, grubby and with a sort of monkey face – jumped down and held out his hand.

"Good to see you, Jack, me old mate! Wondered where you'd got to."

Cabby ignored the hand and I noticed that his expression was one of intense dislike.

"This is Sid Bowcock, Nipper," he said. "Most people call him the Runt. He tells porky pies and he's a tea leaf, so stay away from him and keep your kit locked up when he's about."

It took me a moment to work out that Cabby was saying that the man was a liar and a thief.

"Nah, then, Jacky boy, that's not very friendly, is it?" the Runt replied. An unpleasant, threatening leer spread across his face. "Y'know, the old crowd talks about you a lot – wonder why you pulled the old vanishing trick on them. Like to meet up with you again, a lot of them – just say the word, and I'll fix it for you."

The next second Cabby had him bent backwards over the ship's rail, which was very low at that point.

"You keep your trap shut!" he hissed. "Open it and you'll find out how dangerous this deck is on a dark night. Once you're overboard, you'll be a goner – understand?"

"All right, keep yer wig on!" yelped the Runt in alarm. "I know when to keep shtum. You know me – I'd never grass up a mate!"

"Oh, yes, I know you," said Cabby, hauling him back in-board. "Now, sling your hook!"

"What was all that about?" I asked as the Runt scuttled off.

"You don't want to know, Nipper," Cabby replied, with a hint of sadness in his voice. "You just don't want to know."

Once again, I sensed that Cabby was trying to hide something. He was right about one thing, though – the Runt quickly made himself unpopular. Although he washed, he always looked dirty, sweated a lot and gave off an unpleasant smell. What made this worse was his habit of pushing his face close to yours when he spoke to you. He also enjoyed stirring up trouble between people, although we soon became used to his ways.

Our mail caught up with us again. There was an interesting letter from Dad, containing cuttings from German newspapers that Sir Edmund Emerson, his friend in Naval Intelligence, had obtained from sources in neutral Sweden. They showed pictures of Adolf Hitler presenting Lieutenant Commander Klaus von Schleigen with the Knights' Cross, one of Germany's highest decorations. In the background was a U-boat conning tower with a crowned wolf painted on the side. There was also a photograph of a warship sinking, said to have been taken through the U-boat's periscope. The enclosed translation said that the award was made for the sinking of a British cruiser and a destroyer in circumstances of extreme danger, from which von Schleigen had extricated his boat with great skill and daring. Sir Edmund thought otherwise.

"The fact is that *Anubis* was a very old cruiser," he wrote. "If it had not been for the War she would have been sold for scrap. Her Captain insists that she struck a stray mine and was not torpedoed. It looks as though von Schleigen was in the area and did try to put a torpedo into one of her escorting destroyers that had gone alongside to take off the cruiser's crew. The torpedo actually struck the sinking *Anubis*. The destroyer's bows were seriously damaged by the explosion, but she managed to make port. When a second destroyer counter-attacked with depth charges, von Schleigen made off.

"It seems to me that he is proving to be a disappointment to his masters. His record of sinkings falls well below the average, and this is a matter of concern for the Nazi Party, who wish to make a hero of him. I suspect that this phoney award ceremony is part of the plan. However, I think it is safe to assume that in private he has been told to do a great deal better. No doubt we'll be hearing more of him."

I decided to keep these papers together in case they were

ever needed and I stored them carefully in my locker. Shortly after this, we began to make ready for sea again. After what the Captain had said, I knew that the months ahead would be difficult, but I little suspected just how bad they would be.

At times throughout the months that followed I truly thought that we might lose the War. There were fewer escorts to protect the convoys – as the Captain had predicted – and because the enemy now possessed the French and Norwegian ports, the U-boats were not only present in greater numbers, but also capable of operating further out into the Atlantic. Our trips therefore became longer, leaving us on the edge of exhaustion for much of the time.

Always present during the day were the Condors, circling the convoys and reporting their progress. At night the U-boats, operating in groups called wolf packs, would close in on the surface, penetrate the lines between the merchant ships and torpedo several of them. Sometimes we would lose as much as a third of a convoy in one trip. Knowing how long it took to build a merchant ship, I began to feel that the enemy was sinking them faster than we could launch them, and at the same time building U-boats faster than we could sink them. When, later in the War, I spoke to some captured U-boat men, they described this period as their "happy time", and I could understand why. We felt a terrible frustration at not being able to hit back effectively, for by the time we responded to an attack, the enemy had vanished into the night. Perhaps the unhappiest man on the ship was Pingy. On the rare occasions that his Asdic did produce a faint echo, it disappeared almost immediately. Little did we know at the time that it was the effectiveness of Asdic that had forced the enemy to attack on the surface, for their own protection.

I saw many ships die. A sinking ship is always a tragic sight, but the end for many of them was truly terrible. Most take a little time to go down, enabling much of the crew who survived the torpedo explosion to take to their boats. Not so *Prince Madoc*, which went down during an eastbound convoy. I saw the explosion as the torpedo hit, sending up a great column of water as high as her funnel. Flames appeared aboard her, then a second explosion blew the side out of her. Within seconds she had rolled on to her beam ends and, still moving, slid beneath the waves.

"She was a collier," commented Mr Swinson. "Very dangerous ships to serve aboard. They don't have bulkheads between the cargo holds like a conventional ship – just shifting boards to stop the coal moving about. If the coal starts to move you've got a real problem on your hands, because it can cause a list from which you'll never recover."

"But surely she wouldn't have survived two torpedo hits, anyway, sir?" I queried.

"As far as I could see, she was only hit once," he replied.

"The other danger with colliers is coal dust, which is highly explosive. The torpedo started fires and sent up clouds of the stuff. That caused the second explosion. When the sea poured in she began to list, the coal shifted, and that was that."

We steamed over the area where *Prince Madoc* had gone down, looking for survivors. There was nothing but a film of coal dust spreading over the surface, and the usual flotsam sent up by a sunken ship. It had all happened so quickly that she had carried her entire crew to the bottom of the ocean with her.

Tankers, on the other hand, could become an inferno, but took a long time to sink because they were subdivided into many tanks to prevent their liquid cargo swilling in any direction. Dad had always said that fire at sea is one of the most feared of all perils, but not even he, in all his long years of experience, had ever seen men jumping from a tanker's deck into a sea that was already aflame with fuel escaping from ruptured tanks. Yet, despite torpedo damage and fire, some tankers did survive. We were nearing home with an eastbound convoy when we overtook one, limping along at about five knots. Commander Kemp spoke to her through the loudhailer. She was *Santa Isadora* and had a remarkable story to tell. While sailing with a previous convoy, she had been torpedoed and set ablaze. The crew took to the boats, which became separated during the night. After two days adrift, the boat containing the second mate, the chief engineer and a dozen others had sighted their ship again. She was still afloat and the fires had all but burned themselves out. A Jacob's ladder was banging against the side of the hull in a heavy swell. With difficulty, they climbed this and, after hours of work, succeeded in starting the engines again.

I soon lost count of the survivors we took aboard during those months. Most were British, but there were many other nationalities as well, including French, Belgian, Dutch, Danish, Norwegian, Greek, Indian, Chinese and West Indian. Sometimes, they covered every flat surface above and below deck until they could be transferred. Every blanket and every item of spare clothing from the ship's slop chest would be pressed into use. Some had sustained terrible injuries or burns, some came aboard covered from head to foot in fuel oil, and some were stark naked. Many were in a state of severe shock. Despite the mugs of hot, sweet tea we gave them, they would sit with chattering teeth, staring ahead, shrouded in blankets. These were the sort of men I had known for as long as I could remember, much the same as Dad's crew on old *Antigua Moon*. I had the greatest admiration for their courage, for despite their ordeal, they would find themselves new ships and go to sea again. Some of those we rescued had already been torpedoed once. Sadly, for those with fatal injuries or burns, or those who had swallowed too much fuel oil, we could only keep them as comfortable as possible for the little time they had left to live. I heard the Captain perform the Burial at Sea service so often that I knew the words by heart.

Saddest of all were those for whom we arrived too late. Picking up survivors took time, and if several ships were lost on the same night it might be an hour or more before we reached the site of the last sinking. Life jackets were fitted with small, battery-powered red lights. In winter we would approach a cluster of such lights only to find that those men still in the water, and even some in the crammed lifeboats, had frozen to death. There was something eerie about them as they bobbed up and down, their unseeing eyes in faces turned blue or black. We left them to the sea, for we had little enough space aboard for the living, and none for the dead. I wondered how many of these men had fallen victim to von Schleigen, who loved a sitting target as long as it presented no threat to him.

Despite all this tragedy and loss of life, good news began to reach us from elsewhere. Fighting against terrific odds, the RAF's Fighter Command had defeated every German attempt to gain air superiority over southern England. By the autumn, it was clear that Hitler's planned invasion stood no chance of success, although the Luftwaffe was bombing our cities, including Liverpool, by night. In November the Fleet Air Arm crippled the Italian battle fleet with a torpedo attack on its base, and the following month the heavily outnumbered British Army in Egypt inflicted a severe defeat on the Italians at Sidi Barrani.

Arum had a small success of her own, too. We were used to single Condors shadowing our convoys, but as more of them became available they began to launch attacks of their own, sometimes in groups of six. They would come in from astern, flying at masthead height along the lines of ships, machine gunning and dropping their bombs. These tactics were effective and cost us more ships, for a direct hit with a 500-pound bomb could cause fatal damage to a small vessel, while the blast from an exploding near miss would be enough to blow in hull plating below the water line.

On this occasion we saw the attack start to develop. We were in our usual station astern of the convoy, and watched as the Condors lost height and took up the line-ahead formation, knowing that they would commence their run at the convoy as soon as they were directly behind it.

"Stand by, Mr Merredew!" shouted the Captain from the rear of the bridge. "It looks as though you'll have some customers very shortly!"

"Aye aye, sir!"

The leading aircraft made its turn towards us, heading for the centre column of ships. Behind him, the rest of the Condors wheeled round, fanning out as they decided which column they were going to attack. At Mr Merredew's instructions, the gun layers lined up on the leader, while he personally set the angle of elevation at which they would open fire.

Flying at over 200 miles per hour, the Condor grew bigger every second. Flames flickered from its top and belly turrets as they opened fire. I ducked as bullets cracked passed us or went whining off the ship's steel plating. I heard Mr Merredew shout the order to fire and the Vickers broke into a continuous roar. Together, the four guns pumped out no less than 2,800 rounds per minute, each round travelling at a speed of 2,600 feet per second. I raised my head and saw the Condor fly straight into this wall of flying metal. It seemed to stagger as pieces flew off its nose, then it veered off to starboard. The anti-aircraft gunners followed it round, lacing its length with fire before they turned to the next target. As it passed I could see that the nose was in tatters, while the perspex of the cockpit and upper and lower turrets had been shattered. Then the two Lewis guns on the bridge joined in. Flames began to erupt from the base of the aircraft's port wing, licking hungrily at the fuselage as they spread. The Condor went into a steep banking turn to starboard but began to lose height steadily. We cheered as, a mile away, its wing clipped the waves before plunging into the sea with a mighty splash.

Alarmed by their leader's reception, the rest of the Condors took evasive action to avoid our guns. As a result, their bombs burst harmlessly in the sea between the lines of ships. One received a dose of anti-aircraft fire from the sloop on the port side of the convoy and turned for home with smoke trailing from an engine, followed by his companions.

"Commodore signalling, sir," said Slim.

The Commodore was always a retired naval officer of senior rank who travelled aboard one of the merchant ships and, among other duties, was responsible for ensuring that the merchant captains understood and carried out the escort commander's instructions.

"GOOD SHOOTING *ARUM*. THAT GAVE THEM SOMETHING TO THINK ABOUT. Message ends, sir."

"Reply: THANKS. MAYBE THEY'LL BE LESS COCKY NEXT TIME," commented the Captain, then turned to me. "Rogers, my compliments to Mr Merredew and tell him and his team from me that they've done a first-class job."

The anti-aircraft gunners grinned from ear to ear when I delivered the message. They were the ship's heroes and even the Runt, who was one of those responsible for maintaining the supply of ammunition to the guns, received a pat on the back. Mr Merredew's reaction was one of quiet satisfaction.

"It seems as though I've started to earn my pay at last," he said, smiling to himself.

I think this proved to be a turning point for him. He had earned the crew's respect, and with this his self-confidence grew. In the years that followed he became a very capable officer.

We had begun to operate regularly from Gladstone Dock in Liverpool. Early in 1941 we berthed there after delivering a convoy. The following day the Captain sent for me.

"I understand that you have ambitions to become a signaller, Rogers," he said. "You have completed the necessary sea time and I'm sending you on the appropriate course at the Navy's Signals School."

"Thank you, sir," I replied. Then the thought struck me that I would be leaving behind all the good friends I had made, including Slim, Cabby, Pingy and Sparks. "If possible I'd like to come back to this ship, sir," I added.

"You've done well so far, so pass your course, and I'll see what I can do," he said, with the ghost of a smile. "Fail, and I'll see that you spend the rest of the War on the dirtiest garbage scow in Scapa Flow. Understood?"

"Aye aye, sir," I said, and grinned at him. As the ship's Captain he had to keep some distance between himself and the crew, but it was good to know that he still maintained a personal interest in us.

I was granted some leave before my course started. Liverpool had already been the target of numerous attacks by the Luftwaffe and I never failed to be shocked by the damage I saw in the streets. There were empty spaces or piles of rubble where business premises and houses had once been. Other buildings showed signs of fire or bomb damage and a number of familiar landmarks had disappeared. I reached home to find that I had missed Dad by a few days. His new ship usually formed part of convoys delivering supplies to our troops in the Middle East. As the passage through the Mediterranean was too dangerous, these took the much longer route round the Cape of Good Hope, which meant that he was rarely at home. Mother said I was taller but had lost weight. Although strict rationing was in force, she managed to feed me enormous meals. Our garden had been completely dug over and now grew nothing but vegetables. In one corner of it was the humped shape of an Anderson shelter, which had been made very snug and was shared with neighbours during air raids. I found it very difficult to sleep in a bed, although I had looked forward to it for months. I suppose I had become used to my hammock.

After my leave, I journeyed south to Portsmouth. When I reached the barracks in Portsmouth I was directed to K Block, which housed the Signals School. The course was intensive and lasted for several weeks. It covered signalling with flag hoists, sending and receiving in semaphore and Morse code, including use of the signal lamp and buzzer, encoding and decoding, procedures and other subjects. Fortunately, Slim had told me what to expect and given me some coaching during our off-duty hours. The course ended with oral examinations. The results were announced the following day.

"You've passed, Rogers," said the Signals Lieutenant in charge of the course. "*Arum* have asked for you back. She's completing a refit at a yard on the Clyde. Hurry and you might catch her."

I was as pleased to learn this as I was to know that I had qualified and could now be classified as an Able Seaman, which meant a modest increase in pay – not that I could spend much of it while we were at sea.

After a long overnight train journey I made my way to the yard. *Arum* was lying in the fitting-out basin. There was something different about her. Her bridge had been extended outwards and above and behind it was a large, strange object that looked like a Chinese lantern, sheathed in canvas. Most of the crew were dangling on cradles over the side, painting the hull in the latest camouflage pattern.

"Gawd strewth, it's Nipper!" shouted Cabby. "Thought we'd got rid of you!"

"No such luck!" added Slim, looking at the Signaller's badge I had sewn on to the sleeve of my uniform. "See you passed the course, mate – well done."

During a break they told me what had been happening while I was away. It seemed from their experience on the last convoy that neither the U-boats nor the Condors were having it all their own way any more. More destroyers and corvettes had become available to escort the convoys and they were pursuing more aggressive tactics against the

U-boats. The RAF Coastal Command was also using long-range aircraft to patrol further out into the Atlantic, where they would attack any surfaced U-boat with bombs and depth charges. In addition, because merchant ships had been issued with machine guns to defend themselves against air attack, the Condors were keeping their distance again, and would only attack stragglers. I said that I had heard on the news that two of Germany's best U-boat commanders had been sent to the bottom and a third had been captured when his boat went down.

"There's plenty more of them out there," commented Cabby, shrugging. "It's just as dangerous as it ever was, and it'll stay that way until we start sinking 'em faster than they can build 'em."

"What's that thing they've installed behind the bridge?" I asked.

"Ah, that's our Radar scanner," replied Sparks, his eyes shining with enthusiasm. "Radar stands for Radio Direction And Ranging. It'll probably put Pingy out of a job – still, Chalky might just let him help in the galley."

"It won't work under water, you idiot!" Pingy protested angrily, little realizing that Sparks was making fun of him. "Working together, Radar and Asdic are intended to cover everything above and below the surface!"

"How does Radar work?" I asked.

"Come on, I'll take you to meet Egghead," said Sparks.

"Real name is Frank Dudley, but he's got a big brain inside his baldy bonce, so we call him Egghead. Talks all sorts of gibberish – even I can't understand him sometimes."

We found Egghead in a dimly lit compartment, staring at a glowing screen and twiddling various knobs. His big shiny head was supported by a skinny neck with a prominent Adam's apple. If I had met him elsewhere I would have taken him for a young clergyman. At length, he finished what he was doing, gave a satisfied grunt and turned to us with a benevolent smile.

"Everything working nicely, Eggy?" asked Sparks. "Tell Nipper here how this Radar thing works, will you?"

"Ah, yes," said Egghead in a cultured voice. "Well, you see, we transmit radio signals on a special frequency right round through 360 degrees. If they strike anything, they're reflected back to us. As it revolves, the scanner above picks them up and the result appears on this screen."

A revolving bar extended from the centre of the screen to its edge. As it passed over various shapes they became briefly brighter.

"Now, here we are, right in the middle," he continued, pointing. "If you study the screen closely you'll see the outline of the dock and ships moving out on the river. It will pick up ships and aircraft over a considerable distance, as well as giving me their range and height. And, of course, it works day and night."

"That's marvellous!" I exclaimed. "It means that any U-boat attacking on the surface will soon find itself in trouble."

"Let's hope so," said Egghead. He raised a long-fingered white hand. I thought he was going to bless us, but instead he simply indicated that he wanted to get on with his work, so we left.

For the first time in many months I felt a sense of optimism and looked forward to getting back to sea. Little did I know that I was about to face a new and totally unexpected danger.

During our next westbound convoy we were able to claim a share in the destruction of a U-boat. Pingy picked it up on the Asdic and we made a depth-charge attack. The submarine evidently survived, for when the water had become more settled he picked it up again, apparently trying to get away from us by diving deep under the convoy. The escorts on the far side were informed. They picked it up on their own Asdic as it emerged beneath them, and they blasted the entire area with their depth charges. We were instructed to join the hunt, although as it burned out we were not needed. Once again, I saw great oily bubbles accompanied by flotsam break the surface, but in far greater quantities than on earlier occasions. Suddenly the U-boat's snout broke the surface at a steep angle, followed by the top of the conning tower. It seemed to hover there for a moment, then vanished below the waves, from which air continued to belch for several minutes. There were no survivors. I did feel guilty about our part in sending men to a terrible death – but I knew that if the U-boat had survived it could have sunk more ships and killed even more of our men.

We now escorted convoys as far west as Newfoundland, which meant that we were at sea for much longer periods. At St John's we refuelled while a large eastbound convoy assembled. As this included several troop ships with Canadian soldiers aboard, it had a large escort. This comprised three cruisers, *Norseman* with 8-inch guns, and *Ariel* and *Astraea* with 6-inch guns, several destroyers and corvettes. Our usual station was well out to starboard of the convoy, where we could give advance warning of the presence of U-boats.

Four days out from St John's, we were proceeding through fog banks in a lazy swell. Sometimes the fog limited visibility to a few hundred yards, and sometimes it lifted, allowing us to see several miles ahead. Nothing much seemed to be happening when suddenly Egghead's voice crackled out of the Radar speaker with a real sense of urgency.

"Large surface vessel, bearing green oh-seven-five, range ten miles, estimated speed thirty knots, course due north, sir!"

Mr Rooney, the First Lieutenant, was Officer of the Watch. He responded immediately by pressing the Action Stations button. Within seconds the ship was like a disturbed ant hill. I watched the 4-inch gun crew run forward, pulling on their anti-flash hoods and steel helmets as they did so. The Captain arrived on the bridge and was quickly informed of the unexpected contact. He turned to me.

"Make to escort commander: SUSPECTED ENEMY HEAVY SURFACE UNIT BEARING OH-SEVEN-FIVE TEN MILES AND CLOSING FAST. AM INVESTIGATING."

The fog prevented use of the lamp so I ran to the radio room and handed the message to Sparks. He quickly tapped it out on the buzzer and scribbled the response, which I handed to the Captain.

"KEEP ME INFORMED. WILL JOIN YOU SHORTLY."

Commander Kemp read the reply, then flipped open the engine-room voice pipe.

"I want everything you've got, Chief – even if you shake loose every rivet in the ship!"

The telegraph rang to Full Ahead and *Arum* began to surge forward. Soon we were exceeding the 16 knots of which the builders said she was capable. The Captain did a rapid calculation and gave the helmsman a fresh course that would enable us to intercept the intruder. By now I was aware that if the stranger was an enemy surface raider, his guns could do immense damage to the convoy and cause enormous loss of life. We proceeded on the new course for several minutes, during which Egghead's voice continued to report the range and bearing of the other ship. The tension became almost unbearable. Then, without warning, the fog cleared.

"There he is, sir!" shouted Mr Rooney, pointing. Several miles ahead and to starboard was a sleek grey shape, beautiful but full of menace as it raced through the water. The Captain's calculations had been correct and it was obvious that our paths would cross shortly. The First Lieutenant had lowered his binoculars and was leafing through the recognition manual.

"Hipper Class heavy cruiser, sir," he said. "Eight 8-inch and twelve 4.1-inch guns, five inches of armour."

"Right, then – let's go and knock him about a bit," responded the Captain, his face expressionless. He leant forward over the rail and shouted to the 4-inch gun crew: "Your best shooting, if you please, Mr Rutherford. There's a dirty great Jerry coming up ahead and I want to give him a bloody nose. Open fire as soon as you're in range."

"Aye aye, sir!"

"Hoist our battle ensign, will you?" the Captain said, turning to Slim. "We may as well be properly dressed for the occasion."

"Aye aye, sir!" Slim replied. "Give us a hand, Nipper."

We pulled the ensign from its place in the flag locker, hoisted it on the halyard and broke the bundle with a jerk. Huge and magnificent, it began to stream in the wind of our passage.

"That's the Nelson Touch for you," said Slim with a note of resignation in his voice. "Looks as though our mothers' favourite sons are going to go out in a blaze of glory."

By now I had learned to live with the presence of U-boats

and Condors, but the odds we faced at this moment were impossible. I knew that even a single hit with a 4.1-inch shell could do terrible damage to *Arum*, while that of an 8-inch would destroy her. I was so terrified that my legs began to shake. I was grateful to Commander Kemp when he broke the tension by giving me something to do.

"Make to escort commander: HIPPER CLASS HEAVY CRUISER ON CONVERGING COURSE WITH CONVOY. AM ENGAGING."

The Captain's face broke into a wry smile as he read the reply: ON WAY. DON'T BE GREEDY SAVE SOME FOR US.

Below, on the foredeck, I could see Cabby hunched in the layer's seat of the gun and the ammunition carriers waiting with shells in their arms. Mr Rutherford was methodically calculating the range. The enemy seemed to be paying us no attention at all.

"Either we're too small for him to have spotted us, or he doesn't think we're worth bothering about," commented Mr Rooney, as though he had read my thoughts.

"Then we must change his mind," responded the Captain, and leaned forward over the rail. "As soon as you're ready, Mr Rutherford."

"Shoot!" barked the Gunnery Officer. Cabby took his time, allowing for the pitch and roll of the ship. The gun banged and a waft of hot, expended cordite blew back across the bridge. I watched the red trace in the base of the shell as it sped towards the target. A fountain of water erupted, some distance short of the enemy. Mr Rooney ordered a correction and the gun barked again. This time the shell fell much closer to the target. Before we could get off a third shot I saw a series of orange flashes appear at different points along the cruiser's hull. Seconds later there came a sound like tearing cloth and six shells fell close together some distance astern of us.

"He's using his 4.1s – probably doesn't want to waste his precious 8-inch ammunition on us," commented Mr Rooney.

"Looks that way – nicely grouped together, though," replied the Captain. "I think we'll throw his aim off a little."

He ordered the helm to be put hard to port and told the engine room to make smoke. As the ship heeled during her turn, oil was injected into the burners below. Impenetrable black smoke began to belch from the funnel as we turned in a circle. I heard another salvo land harmlessly in the sea somewhere in the fog we had left behind us.

"Ready, Mr Rutherford," called the Captain. "We've nearly come full circle. I can let you have two more shots, then we're going hard a' starboard."

The gun fired again as we emerged from our own smoke. I didn't see where the shell landed, but as the enemy was now much closer I guessed that it had passed over him. However, just seconds after we fired our second shot I saw a bright red flash high up on the cruiser's control tower. I heard the gun crew cheer, then we turned away again.

"That made his teeth rattle!" said the Captain with a satisfied grin. Another enemy salvo screamed over our heads, making us duck. Then we turned back on ourselves by going to port, hoping to upset the cruiser's aim still further. When we emerged from the smoke again the whole situation had changed. *Norseman*, guns blazing, was coming up astern of the enemy, while *Ariel* and *Astraea* were closing in from ahead. There were splashes all round the German cruiser and red flashes where shells struck home on her hull and upper works. Her return fire, split between several targets, seemed to have no effect. I realized that she had probably had enough, for she began to make smoke and turned away to the south with our own cruisers in hot pursuit. They gave up the chase as soon as the faster German ship was out of range. As they returned a light began blinking on *Norseman's* bridge.

"That's our number – you take it," said Slim.

"*ARUM*. NEXT TIME PICK ON SOMEONE YOUR OWN SIZE," I read out.

"Reply: WILL DO. HOPE WE DIDN'T SPOIL YOUR FUN," said the Captain, chuckling.

We secured from Action Stations and our watch went to dinner. Everyone was in high spirits, for now we could boast that the little *Arum* had emerged unscathed from a fight with a German heavy cruiser.

"A most satisfactory outcome," intoned Egghead, as though he had just concluded a marriage ceremony.

"You've got to admire the old man," said Sparks, referring to the Captain. "The Jerries must have thought we were raving mad, going for them like that. By the time our cruisers came up they didn't know which way to turn, so they cleared off!"

A long time afterwards, when the War was over, I learned that we had been fighting *Ludendorff*. She had returned to Germany in her damaged state without sinking a single merchant vessel. It seemed that the one hit we scored had penetrated her gunnery control centre, putting it out of action. This explained why her gunnery was so bad during the rest of the engagement, and why she had turned tail and run.

When we reached Liverpool at the end of May I was horrified by what I saw. For a full week, the Luftwaffe had mounted a concentrated bombing offensive, hoping to put the port out of action once and for all. In the Bootle area, behind our berth in Gladstone Dock, whole streets of houses had been obliterated. In the city itself large areas had been flattened or stood ruined and gutted. The docks had sustained serious damage, but not as serious as the enemy would have liked, and they were coming back into action.

We were out again almost as soon as we had refuelled and

taken on fresh supplies. For the rest of the year we continued with our apparently endless routine of convoy escort, occasionally losing ships but keeping the enemy at bay with depth-charge attacks whenever a contact was made. I began to feel that this was how I was going to spend the rest of my life. There were, however, two important developments in our war. We were at sea on 23 June when the ship's tannoy speakers crackled into life.

"D'ye hear there! This is the Captain. I have just been informed that yesterday Hitler launched an invasion of the Soviet Union. Our country is no longer alone. We may not care for the way the Russians run their affairs, but they are now our allies and in my opinion they will be tough nuts to crack. I believe that Hitler has made the worst mistake of his life.

"One other thing. I am pleased to tell you that Lieutenant Rutherford and Able Seaman Pearson have been mentioned in Dispatches for their part in our action against the enemy cruiser. Congratulations to them both."

We all cheered and slapped Cabby on the back. A new voice came through on the tannoy.

"This is the First Lieutenant. The Captain has omitted to mention that he has been awarded the Distinguished Service Cross for the same engagement. He has accepted this on behalf of the whole ship's company. There is no doubt that we distracted the enemy long enough for our own cruisers to come out and give him a good hiding. Well done everyone. That is all."

We cheered again, glad that *Arum* was making a name for herself. We felt a great sense of satisfaction that we were doing our job well, although we all knew that months, and possibly years, of constant vigilance, of periods of intense fear alternating with boredom, of gales, snow and ice, of being unbearably cold, wet and overcrowded, lay ahead of us before we could claim to have driven the enemy from the Atlantic for good.

The end of the first week in December found us in Liverpool again. The mail came aboard and I started to read a long and interesting letter from Dad, telling me of his own experiences. One paragraph was of particular interest:

I've heard from my old friend at Naval Intelligence again. He says that now we have disposed of the real U-boat aces, men like Kretschmer, Prien and Schepke, the Nazi Propaganda Ministry is giving von Schleigen all the publicity they can. His total of merchant ship tonnage sunk is rising slowly. However, when all the bits and pieces of information are put together it seems that rather than attacking escorted convoys, he prefers trailing along behind them and picking off isolated stragglers. There are never any survivors from these vessels. Significantly, fragments of ships' boats, bodies and so on, have been found at the scene of the sinkings. This suggests that he is using his gun to blow the boats apart. Poor devils.

The mess-deck radio had been providing a background of music while we read our letters. Suddenly the music stopped and the newsreader's voice came through.

"Here is an important announcement. Early this morning aircraft of the Imperial Japanese Navy launched a treacherous and unprovoked attack on the United States' Pacific Fleet in its base at Pearl Harbor in the Hawaiian Islands. American losses in warships and men are said to be heavy. Following this attack, Japan formally declared war on the United Kingdom and the United States. Germany is also understood to have declared war on the United States."

There was a stunned silence while we absorbed this completely unexpected news. Finally, Slim broke the silence.

"All right, so it will take a bit longer for us to finish this war. Hitler's already got us and the Russians on his hands – now he's taking on America, the biggest industrial power in the world. In the long run he'll lose, and then we'll deal with the Japs."

With America on our side, I was sure that we would win. I was confident that things would get better soon. In fact, they got worse.

1942

The third winter of the War was just as unpleasant as those that had gone before. Bad weather usually kept the U-boats down, but it also meant that everyone on the bridge was soaked and frozen within minutes of going on watch. Things could have been much worse for us, however – men serving on warships engaged in escorting convoys to northern Russia told me that they had a far harder time of it than we did. These convoys were necessary because the Russians had sustained a series of terrible defeats in the months following the German invasion of their country. They had to be kept supplied with the tanks, guns and munitions that would enable them to go on fighting. In winter, the edge of the Arctic ice shelf moved south, leaving only a narrow passage of open water to the north of Norway, from which the convoys bound for Murmansk and Archangel in the Soviet Union came under constant attack from U-boats and the Luftwaffe's torpedo bomber squadrons. Then there was the bitter weather they had to endure – so bad that ice had to be chipped off upperworks and rigging to prevent ships capsizing because they had become top-heavy. It was said that in those regions the water was so cold that a man wouldn't survive for more than 30 seconds in it. In such circumstances, therefore, we felt we had no right to complain – not that anyone did, for conditions were the same for all of us and a moaner on the mess deck got very little sympathy.

By this time, Slim left most of the lamp signalling to me, although he remained at my elbow to make sure that I got it right. In this way I became more efficient at my job. He had told me that every signaller has his own technique – like a personal signature –and as time went by I began to recognize individual signallers and put names to them when we were tied up alongside their ships in harbour.

One day Mr Parry, the Chief Engineer, appeared on the bridge. He told the Captain that the constant heavy weather had put a serious strain on the engines. He explained that one of the propeller shaft's main bearings was about to collapse and would not stand up to the return trip across the Atlantic. As a result of this, we were ordered to proceed to Boston Navy Yard for repairs, after we had delivered our convoy to Halifax, Nova Scotia.

Wherever we went in Boston we were treated like royalty by the Americans. After the strict rationing at home, we were able to tuck in to the sort of food we had not seen in such quantities since before the War, including huge steaks and ice cream in many flavours that we had never even heard of. We were walking back to the ship one evening when who should I see coming towards us but Roddy Maguire, Dad's old boatswain on *Antigua Moon*. At first he didn't recognize me, but when the penny finally dropped we stood there laughing, shaking hands and slapping each other on the back.

"What are you doing in Boston?" I asked.

"They took me on as boatswain on *Barbados Moon*," he replied. "Now she's on the bottom, a couple of hundred miles south of here. I tell you, Peter, being torpedoed once is bad enough, but twice is too much. Still, the sea is all I know and I'm looking for another ship."

I was shocked to hear this as, although we lost a ship from time to time, most of those we escorted across the Atlantic reached their destinations safely. Roddy shook his head when I told him this.

"True enough," he said, "but once the convoy disperses we're on our own. Just now, the Americans are more worried about the Japs in the Pacific than they are about the U-boats in the Atlantic. The Jerries know this and have started operating off the American coast and in the Caribbean. There is no blackout here, so all a U-boat has to do is lie low during the day, pop up at night, and there we are, silhouetted against the bright lights. We're sitting ducks."

"Why doesn't the American Navy operate a convoy system like we do?"

"Well, they're talking about it and I dare say it will

come to that, but at the moment they say they haven't enough escorts."

We chatted for a while about other things, then went our separate ways. I was horrified that after all our efforts to protect merchant ships during their long crossings, many of them were still being sunk almost within sight of their destinations. Much later, I learned that the Allies had lost many thousands of tons of shipping during this period, which captured U-boat crews described as their second "happy time". Against this, shipyards in Britain, Canada and America were turning out ships of all types as fast as they could. The Americans' wartime version of a cargo vessel was a very simple design. I first saw one while I was talking to one of the workmen in the Navy Yard.

"We call 'em Liberty Ships," he commented. "Just a hull, engine, smokestack and propeller – an' not much else besides. Sure ain't pretty an' there's nothin' fancy about 'em, but they do the job an' that's all we want 'em for."

"How long do they take to build?" I asked.

"Oh, we go in for a lot of mass production over here," he replied. "I guess it takes a few weeks, but once the teams of guys an' gals workin' on 'em get used to the job they'll speed up a lot. Right now, when one's launched they put down a new keel in her place the same day."

His answer astonished me, as I had always been under the impression that it took many months to build and fit out a ship of that size.

As soon as our repairs were complete we regretfully left friendly Boston and its virtually un-rationed food.

By the time we resumed our monotonous escort duty spring had arrived. For much of our passage both ways we had daily sightings of Allied aircraft, flying not just from home, but also from Iceland, Canada and the United States. Sometimes we exchanged signals with them. It was a great comfort to see them, as we knew that they would instantly attack any U-boat they sighted with bombs and depth charges, as well as giving us early warning of their presence. The Captain said that as longer-range aircraft came into service, the remaining area in the mid-Atlantic would also be covered.

As spring began to turn into summer, the nights in the northern latitudes grew shorter. It was about 04:00 one morning when Egghead reported a contact dead ahead at about five miles' range. We went to Action Stations. At first the contact was difficult to identify, even through binoculars, but at length the Captain reached a decision.

"It's a U-boat charging her batteries on the surface," he said. "Keeping a sloppy lookout by all accounts, or he'd have vanished as soon as he spotted us."

He ordered the gun crew to stand by as we began to creep up on the target. I saw Cabby making slight adjustments to the lay of the gun as Mr Rutherford allowed for the decreasing range. Normally, the escorts hunted as a team, but as we were some miles ahead of the convoy and none of the other warships were nearby I think that the Captain had decided to take advantage of the opportunity offered before the enemy could slip away.

"Now, Mr Rutherford!" he called. "Shoot!"

The gun banged. I watched the shell's red trace as it sped straight for the target and saw a vivid red flash as it struck home.

"A hit!" someone shouted, and we all cheered.

The gun banged again, but I didn't see where the shell landed.

"U-boat submerging, sir," said the lookout. As the conning tower disappeared beneath the waves the Asdic began to pick up echoes from the submarine.

"Target bearing left, sir!" said Pingy's voice in the speaker.

We altered course to conform with the enemy, whose track was clearly marked by a continuous slick of oil, like the trail of blood left by a wounded animal.

"Stand by, depth charges!" ordered the Captain. As we reached the end of the slick he pressed the release buzzer. The depth charges went rolling over the stern and the usual eruptions of water were thrown up as they exploded far below. We immediately went about to pass over the target area. In the excitement of the moment I was dimly aware that the return echoes on the Asdic had ceased.

"U-boat surfacing, sir!" shouted the lookout. As the

sinister grey shape broke the surface our 4-inch swung towards it. The bridge machine gun opened fire. A figure appeared in the enemy's conning tower, waving something white.

"Cease firing!" ordered the Captain. "He's surrendering – lower scramble nets."

Oil was flowing out of the U-boat's riven hull in quantities I had never seen before. As we slowed to a stop some 20 yards from the enemy, men began jumping into the sea and swimming towards us. Before all of them could be hauled aboard, the U-boat had taken its final dive. Oil continued to bubble to the surface from its last resting place. The survivors, about 20 of them, looked just as wretched as those we rescued from our own merchant ships. Their Captain was brought up on to the bridge, where he and Commander Kemp exchanged salutes and shook hands. The German seemed resigned to his fate.

"My compliments on your gunnery, Captain," he said in excellent English. "I am sorry to say that our Radar is not so efficient at picking up surface vessels, or we should have made good our escape. Still that is the fortune of war."

"As you say, Captain," replied Commander Kemp. "I could not help noticing that your boat is not fitted with torpedo tubes, by the way."

"That is correct," said the German. "We are a *milch kuh*, a milk cow, you would say – that is, a submarine tanker.

Our task was to refuel the fighting U-boats and provide them with any torpedoes they need. This would allow them to remain on patrol for longer periods. Now, some of our comrades will have to go home early, I think."

"No doubt that will please a few of them," commented the Captain, drily.

When the watch changed I found the rest of the prisoners under guard on the mess deck. Cleaned up and given fresh clothes from the ship's slop chest, they sat gulping mugs of hot tea. They were the first Germans I had seen at close quarters. Apart from their beards, pallor from lack of sun and long hair combed back, they looked remarkably like us. One of them, realizing that the War was over for him, showed me a photo of his family in an attempt to be friendly. His English, like the Captain's, was remarkably good.

"Do you know a U-boat commander named von Schleigen?" I asked him. A wary look came into his eyes. One of the other prisoners barked something at him and he refused to answer. I realized that some Nazis would be present in any prisoner of war camp and that if he had said too much there would be possibly fatal, consequences for him. I decided to stop questioning him. As soon as we were able, we transferred the prisoners to ships better able to hold them.

A month later we learned that Cabby had been awarded the Distinguished Service Medal for his part in the destruction of the U-boat. He took a lot of leg-pulling in good part, but was less than pleased when we got a delivery of newspapers, some of which contained accounts of the action, naming him as *Arum*'s gun layer. He became withdrawn for a while and didn't come ashore with the rest of us whenever we docked in Liverpool, making all sorts of excuses to stay aboard. I noticed, too, that the Runt had begun making pointed remarks to him, always with an unpleasant smirk. Cabby would never have stood for that normally, but now he hardly reacted at all, although I could see the anger boiling up inside him.

The situation came to a head when someone's money went missing. Among other things, this meant a locker search. We all feared that the thief might have planted the money in our lockers to save himself. To our intense relief, it was discovered by CPO Nobby Clarke in the Runt's locker, hidden inside some clothing. At first the Runt claimed he'd won it in a card game, but when his story fell apart under the Captain's close questioning, he changed tack and said that Cabby must have put it there because he had a grudge against him. No one believed him and he received a severe punishment. In addition, the rest of us arranged for Cabby and the Runt to be left on their own for a while on the mess deck. When we returned, the Runt was groaning in a corner, mouthing that he would fix it for Cabby so that he would wish he had never been born. Once again, I wondered what had happened between them to make them such enemies.

Most of the time we were too involved in our own war to know much about what was going on elsewhere. However, from the BBC's news bulletins and the newspapers that reached us during the first half of the year we knew that the War wasn't going at all well for the Allies anywhere. But slowly things started to change. First, the Americans sank four of Japan's best aircraft carriers in a single day. Next, in North Africa, Rommel's apparently victorious army was fought to a standstill at El Alamein, then decisively defeated after our own Eighth Army had recovered its strength. A little later, a large part of the German Army was surrounded and trapped at a place called Stalingrad in the Soviet Union.

It was during early December that I sensed things were beginning to go our way in the Atlantic as well. As our outward-bound convoy was forming up in Liverpool Bay it was joined by an odd-looking merchant ship with a ramp between the bows and the foremast. At the rear end of the ramp was the unmistakable shape of a Hurricane fighter aircraft. It was Mr Swinson's watch and I asked him what she was.

"She's a CAM ship," he replied. "Stands for Catapult-Aircraft Merchant ship. If a Condor appears the Hurricane does a catapult-assisted take-off and then the Jerries have got a fight on their hands. They've been about for a few months now, although we've not had one with us before."

I couldn't see how the Hurricane could land back on board the CAM ship once it had done its job. It wasn't fitted with floats like a seaplane, and there was no crane to hoist it out of the water anyway.

"Once it's airborne, that's it," Mr Swinson explained. "Either it gets the Condor or the Condor gets it. If the Hurricane wins, the pilot can only ditch ahead of the nearest friendly ship and hope he gets picked up. Not a job I'd care for."

I saw what he meant just a few days later. We were about 400 miles out and the convoy had just completed one of its periodic zigzag changes of course, intended to confuse U-boats, when three Condors appeared. They were circling just out of range, waiting to pounce on any straggler, when a sudden blast of smoke and flame drew my attention to the CAM ship. Assisted by the rocket-propelled sledge on which it rested, the Hurricane roared along the ramp and took to the air over the ship's bows. It climbed steadily until it was lost to view in the sun's glare.

"There he goes!" shouted Slim.

The Hurricane, its eight machine guns blazing, was swooping down on one of the Condors in a long, steep dive. Blinded by the sun, the German gunners were unable to react in time. Pieces flew off their aircraft as it staggered under the impact. The Hurricane pulled up from its dive, banked away, then turned in to latch on to the German aircraft, the pilot of which was trying to take violent evasive action. It was too late. Once again the Condor was lashed by machine gun fire. Trailing smoke and flames, it lost height and plunged into the sea.

We all cheered, but the Hurricane pilot had not quite finished. He went into a steep climb and vanished into the sun again. By now, the two remaining Condors had come together for their mutual protection and seemed to have lost interest in the convoy. They began to climb, but seemed uncertain what to do next. I could imagine their gunners nervously searching the sky above for another attack. Suddenly I spotted the Hurricane. It had dived on the opposite side of the convoy to the enemy and was now approaching at maximum speed, just above masthead height.

"There he goes again!" I exclaimed as it roared directly over our heads. It dropped to sea level, almost skimming the waves, then climbed steeply to put a long burst into the belly of one of the Condors. As it banked away, both enemy aircraft turned for home, one of them with an engine ablaze. The Hurricane flew the length of the convoy and back again, waggling it wings triumphantly. Its pilot then reduced speed and set it down as gently as possible in the sea, about a mile ahead of us. By the time we reached the spot the aircraft had sunk and he was sitting in his yellow rubber dinghy, grinning and waving.

He was hauled aboard and came up on to the bridge, peeling off his flying helmet to reveal a head of long blond hair and a cheery grin. We all applauded and he grinned even wider.

"Hello, chaps," he said with a fine disregard of naval discipline as he shook the Captain's hand. "Pilot Officer Jerry Vernon. Hoped to get two of the blighters for you, but I ran out of ammo. Still, one and a half ain't too bad first time out, is it? That first Hun took a nasty header into the drink, what? Talk about a prang! Absolutely wizard! Pity about the old kite, though. Got her tuned up just right – never get another like her. I say, it's pretty cold in that water – don't suppose anyone's got a hip flask of Scotch, have they?"

He stayed with us for the rest of the trip. He never stopped talking, got in everyone's way, poked around in the engine room, pestered Pingy and Egghead to explain what they were doing, and would have fired the 4-inch for fun if Mr Rutherford hadn't stopped him. His good humour was infectious and we were all sorry to see him go. I often wonder what happened to him.

It had been a mixed sort of year for us, but at least it had ended on a high note.

When we returned to Liverpool early in the new year we were ordered across the river to Cammell Lairds shipyard for a further refit. This was going to take a little while to complete and we were all granted leave. Before we split up, Pingy, Sparks, Egghead and I decided to have a drink together. This time Cabby joined us, as it was impossible for him to remain aboard. As we were walking down the gangway, the Runt called after us, "Where are you off to, lads?"

"We're having a couple of wets in the Baltic Fleet," replied Sparks.

"What d'you tell him that for?" asked Cabby in annoyance. "He'll only come and join us – pity to spoil a good party."

The Baltic Fleet was an old pub on Liverpool's Dock Road, named after some naval operations that had taken place during the Crimean War, nearly 90 years earlier. It was used by seamen and dock workers, and we usually dropped in there whenever we were in port. Some of the engine-room staff, who we called the Black Gang because of their grubby working overalls, were already there when we arrived.

About an hour later Slim, Pingy and Sparks had gone to the washroom when the door opened and four men walked in. Their sharply cut suits, flashy ties and big trilby hats were typical of the spivs who pilfered the rationed goods arriving at the docks and then sold them at excessive prices on the black market. Beneath their brilliant hair were sharp, vicious faces. They looked round, spotted Cabby and walked over to us.

"Well, well, if it isn't Jack Pearson," said their leader. He spoke with a strong London accent. His teeth showed in a smile beneath his pencil-slim moustache, but his eyes were as cold and hard as stones. He fingered Cabby's medal ribbon unpleasantly. "Bit of a hero by all accounts, they say. We was all hopin' we'd bump into you sometime, isn't that right, fellers?"

"Look who's just crawled out from under a stone," replied Cabby. He had suddenly become tense and his eyes were as hard as the other man's. "Cyril Robson, his cousin Bert, Slicer Morris and Legs Harris. Long way from home, aren't you, boys?"

"Don't mess us about, Jacky Boy," snarled Cyril. "You've got something of ours an' we want it back. Hand it over, an' all you'll get is good slappin'."

"Yeah, all right," said Cabby, shrugging in apparent resignation. He stood up and called across to the barman. "Ted, hand over that briefcase I asked you to look after, will you?"

There was no briefcase, of course, but the move broke Cyril's concentration. In a swift and sudden move Cabby overturned the heavy, cast-iron table. It landed on Cyril's feet, causing him to yelp with pain. Before he could recover, Cabby had landed a terrific blow in his midriff, completely winding him. Bert rushed at Cabby, but I kicked a bar stool between his legs. He tripped and went down heavily on top of his cousin.

"Nipper, look out!" someone shouted.

Slicer was coming straight for me and I suddenly realized where his nickname came from – because he had a cut-throat razor in his hand. Some instinct told me to close with him before he could use it. He expected me to back off, but I charged at him and punched him. He staggered back against the bar then came at me again with blood streaming from his nose and mouth. At that moment, much to my astonishment, Egghead struck him on the head with a bottle and his knees buckled. Then Egghead himself was attacked by Legs and the two of them ended up in tangle of wrestling limbs on the floor.

At that point the fight became general. What the spivs had not allowed for was that a ship's company is a family, and that if you attack one of its members the rest will come to his defence. Not only did Slim, Pingy and Sparks emerge from the washroom, the Black Gang joined in too and all hell broke loose. Cyril had been knocked flat again when Slim, all 15 stone of him, climbed on to the bar and jumped. He landed on Cyril's chest as the latter tried to struggle to his feet. I thought I heard a rib crack. The rest of the spivs were lying about the place, similarly battered, their sharp suits torn and stained with blood.

The landlord had already telephoned for the police, who arrived just as the fight ended. Deciding that the Londoners had caused the trouble, the police carted them off in the Black Maria van, after making them pay for the damage that had been caused.

"You're a dead man, Jack," croaked Cyril as he was bundled through the door, clutching his chest.

"Disgraceful behaviour," commented Egghead.

"Quite right," agreed the landlord. "We don't want their sort round here."

"That's not quite what I meant," mused Egghead. "I hit a man on the head with a bottle. My father is an Archdeacon and he would be horrified to learn what I have done." A benevolent smile spread across his face. "On the other hand, if I had not acted as I did, young Nipper might have sustained serious injury – and, in the circumstances, I rather enjoyed smiting an obvious Philistine."

Shortly afterwards, most people began to drift away to catch their trains home. Cabby, however, stood uncertainly on the pavement as though wondering what to do. I asked him where he intended to spend his leave.

"Well, I've got some cousins in Peckham and I was going there," he said, thoughtfully. "Just now, though, I don't think anywhere near the Smoke is too healthy for me, so I dunno, mate."

I gladly offered a room at my parents' house and he accepted gratefully. We took a tram home and on the way he explained what had caused the problems leading up to the brawl in the pub.

"It's like this, Nipper. In Poplar – that's my part of London – it's the Robson Boys who are top dogs. There's a lot of 'em and they're well organized. They go in for bank robberies, wages snatches and the like. Don't bother most people, but cross 'em and you'll end up dead in the river. Now in the next manor, it's the Hackney Gang who run things. They'd got a protection racket going – all the pub landlords, café owners and shopkeepers paid them so much a week or their places got done over. Well, they got ambitious and strayed over the border into Poplar. The Robsons didn't like it and fixed a couple of their lads good and proper. After that it was war.

"One night, Abe Greenberg hails my cab and tells me to take him to the Plague Pit – that's the Robsons' boozer. Abe was their solicitor, and very smart he was, too. The law didn't stand a chance against him, he was so good at fixing things. He also laundered the take on their jobs – you know, if they'd nabbed new, numbered bank notes that could be traced, he'd change them for old notes at a price.

"Anyway, I pulled up outside the Plague Pit and Abe went in. I was just about to move off when four or five cars arrived and the entire Hackney Gang piled out and charged into the pub. Next thing, someone comes flying through the window. Inside, I could see blue murder going on – knives, razors, coshes, blood all over the place. Out ran Abe and dived into cab, but two of the Hackney lads were on his tail so he's in one door and out the other. On the way, he dropped his briefcase. I wasn't hangin' about, either, and took off. Later, when I opened the briefcase, I found 35,000 quid inside. I'd never seen so much money in my life. I guessed it was stolen, but temptation got the better of me and I decided to keep it.

"That wasn't clever, because the Robsons were able to trace it to me without any trouble. It seems they were having a share-out that night. They suspected that the Runt, who liked to keep a foot in both camps, had tipped off the Hackney gang. Abe said he'd dropped his briefcase in the cab to stop the Hackney mob getting their hands on it. The Robsons gave me twenty-four hours to come up with the goods, so I had to think fast. I decided to move away – somewhere I could set myself up, where they'd never find me, maybe Australia. I sold the cab for a knock-down price, then had to think what to do with all the money. I didn't want to carry great wad of cash round with me, so I had to convert it into something small and valuable. Jewels crossed my mind, but they were easily lost. In the end I went along to Stanley

Gibbons, the stamp dealers in the Strand, and spent most of it on rare stamps they said would increase in value with time. Most people wouldn't know what they were worth, although you did when you saw them in my locker.

"I was on the train to Southampton to get a passage when I realized that a couple of the Robsons' hard men were watching me from further down the carriage. I gave them the slip by jumping out of the train just as it was leaving one of the stations along the way. Now I knew I was really in trouble. I had to think of somewhere they wouldn't find me. A warship at sea seemed a good idea, so I went to Portsmouth and signed on with the Navy, thinking I'd jump ship as soon as things cooled down. Then the War started, so deserting was out of the question – I didn't want the Navy and the police after me as well as the Robsons, did I? The rest you know."

"Only some of it," I said. "I don't understand how the Robsons knew you were in the Baltic Fleet."

"That's easy, mate. When we berthed, I reckon the Runt got on the blower and told them I was aboard. They sent a team up here and once he knew where we were going he called 'em again. The fact is, Nipper, I'm even more of a marked man after the hiding we gave them in the pub."

I was glad Cabby had told me the full story, but I worried about what might happen next time the Londoners tracked him down. We had an enjoyable leave during which Cabby made himself a welcome guest, bustling about the house doing jobs for Mother that had been neglected while Dad and I were away. Dad also managed a few days at home while he was in port and we had a party to celebrate. He was in good humour but I could tell that the continued strain of waiting for a torpedo to come through the side of his ship was beginning to take its toll on him. His ship had been supplying the Anglo-American army that had landed in French North Africa the previous November. He said that during one trip his convoy had come under attack and a hospital ship had been torpedoed. In fact, she had been outward bound and, apart from the crew, only doctors and nurses were aboard, most of whom had been rescued. He kept saying that if she had been homeward bound, with her wards full of wounded, the loss of life would have been horrific. The incident seemed to prey on his mind a lot.

We returned from leave to find *Arum* transformed. The Vickers machine guns on the bandstand behind the funnel had been replaced by a 2-pounder rapid-fire anti-aircraft gun that gave us longer range and a better punch, and there were several 20-mm Oerlikons positioned about the ship. There was a new Radar scanner circling above the bridge, which Egghead claimed could pick up anything, even targets as small as a ship's boat, and Pingy was delighted with his new Asdic. Strangest of all was a rack of things that looked like upended gas bottles, on the starboard side just forward of the bridge. We were told that this was a weapon called a Hedgehog, which fired depth bombs in a pattern ahead of the ship. In the past, it seemed, U-boats could hear us coming on their hydrophones, anticipate the moment we would release our depth charges, and avoid the worst effects of these by dodging out of our path at the last minute. The Hedgehog bombs were intended to explode around them before they could react, but we would still release our depth charges for good measure.

There had been some changes among those aboard, too. Mr Rooney had left us to command a corvette of his own, Mr Rutherford had become First Lieutenant and Mr Merredew, now a full Lieutenant, was Gunnery Officer. A new Sub-Lieutenant, Mr Leigh, joined the ship. As Cabby had predicted, the Runt failed to return from leave and was posted as a deserter. Months later, we learned that he had been found, badly beaten up, in an East End back alley. It took him some time to recover, after which he was sentenced to a long spell in a naval detention barracks. The general opinion was that he was no loss to us.

We carried out some exercises to get us used to using the Hedgehog, then resumed our apparently endless duties of escorting convoys over to Halifax and back. However, we now had a new confidence in ourselves and our weapons. The convoys were heavily escorted, especially those carrying American troops, and our long-range air cover was being steadily extended along our route. There was still a gap in the mid-Atlantic, but this was sometimes covered by a new sort of vessel, the Merchant Aircraft Carrier, which had replaced the CAM ship. The MACs were fitted with a flight deck, to one side of which was an island bridge – just like a naval aircraft carrier – and they carried four aircraft. They also carried their normal cargo and, apart from the service personnel responsible for the aircraft, they were manned by merchant navy crews and flew the Red Ensign. We were always glad to have one along during the middle of our passage, as the sight of their patrolling aircraft tended to make the U-boats dive deeper, out of harm's way.

Together, air cover and escorts had begun to make life difficult for the enemy. However, they were now operating in wolf packs and still managed to pick off a large number of ships. For the first few months of the year we were even more hard pressed than usual. Then, about May there seemed to be a slow but steady improvement in our fortunes. We began to lose fewer ships and accounted for more U-boats. Whenever one was detected by our patrolling aircraft, it would either be bombed or the escort would close in and hunt it to destruction. In fog, some would try stalking our convoys on the surface, thinking that they were invisible. They weren't, of course, because our

Radar picked them up very quickly, and before they knew it they had several escort vessels on their hands.

Of course, our own contribution to the War occupied all our attention, but it seemed that the War was going well for us elsewhere, too. Later in the year we acquired a film projector and a supply of films that were shown on the mess deck whenever time permitted – which was not often. We got to know them by heart and exchanged them with other corvettes in port. We also got some newsreels that were long out of date but showed the enemy's surrender in North Africa, the invasions of Sicily and Italy, and the Italian surrender. One of our favourites – always greeted with cheers – included footage of Coastal Command aircraft attacking U-boats in the Bay of Biscay on their way to or from their bases in France. The Captain also announced that, for the first time, not only was the tonnage of merchant ships launched greater than that being sunk, but also the number of U-boats sent to the bottom was at an all-time high.

As always, we were constantly active, with little time for sleep or rest, and my memories of this period are a little jumbled. However, I remember one incident vividly. One dark, moonless night, we were about 50 miles off the south-west coast of Iceland and were astern of the convoy, having just rounded up a straggler with engine problems, when Egghead's voice came over the loudspeaker.

"LARGE VESSEL, RED ONE HUNDRED, RANGE SIX MILES, PROCEEDING NORTH, SPEED TEN KNOTS!"

Remembering our action with *Ludendorff*, the Captain immediately sounded Action Stations and informed the escort commander by radio. We reversed course to intercept the strange vessel. Following Egghead's directions, we soon became aware of a distant glow. This resolved itself into a tanker with a well-lit flag of neutral Sweden painted on the side.

"Ask him who he is and where he's going," ordered the Captain, frowning a little. I did so, using the signal lamp. The answer came back quickly:

"WE ARE SWEDISH TANKER NILS GUSTAVSEN ON PASSAGE FROM GALVESTON TO GOTHENBERG."

"He's lying through his teeth," announced the Captain. "He'd be far lower in the water if he had really loaded up with oil at Galveston – agree, Number One?"

"I agree, sir," replied Mr Rutherford. "What's more, why would a neutral be trying to slip through the Denmark Strait between Iceland and Greenland? In fact, if he's genuine, he'd be taking the direct route home, hundreds of miles to the south. My guess is that's he's a Jerry, trying to run the blockade."

"I agree," said the Captain, then turned to me. "Make: HEAVE TO. I AM SENDING A PARTY ABOARD."

"I AM NEUTRAL YOU HAVE NO RIGHT TO STOP ME", came the reply.

The Captain ordered Mr Merredew to put a shot across the stranger's bows and the 4-inch banged. Cabby's aim was so close that the shot probably blistered the tanker's paintwork as it passed. I was told to signal that unless the other ship stopped we would fire into her. A lamp blinked the reply from her bridge.

"NO YOU WILL NOT. I HAVE BRITISH PRISONERS ABOARD. BAD LUCK OLD CHAP."

I had never seen the Captain so angry. He informed the escort commander of the situation and we were ordered to capture the tanker by any means possible. We followed it at a distance for several hours, and although it increased speed and made several alterations of course, we had no difficulty in maintaining contact.

"He's turned due east and is maintaining course, sir," came Egghead's voice.

"Going to hole up in one of the fjords until he thinks the coast is clear," the Captain commented to Mr Rutherford. "Evidently doesn't know how good our Radar is. We'll drop back a little and let him think he's fooled us."

I was sent to fetch a detailed chart of the Icelandic coast. The Captain disappeared into the Radar office with it and emerged again a few minutes later.

"Radar plot shows him entering Lokisfjord," he said, pointing out a long, winding inlet.

"Contact lost, sir," announced Egghead.

"He's disappeared round the bend here," noted the Captain. "He's screened from Radar by these mountains. We'll give him a few hours to settle down, then go in after him."

"You remember that he's got British prisoners aboard, sir?" asked Mr Rutherford, a cautionary note in his voice.

"Yes, and I'm counting on them being held in one of his empty tanks, well away from the superstructure, where they might try to take over. If necessary, I'll use the Oerlikons to keep the Jerries quiet, but nothing heavier. You'll lead the boarding party, Number One. Once you're aboard, ignore the temptation to go for the bridge. It's the engine room we're after – once that's in our hands there's nothing he can do."

"Aye aye, sir. I'll detail the boarders now."

The boarding party consisted of Mr Rutherford, Mr Merredew, CPO Clarke, Cabby and me, along with about 20 others. The party was divided into two groups, with Mr Rutherford in overall command. Mr Merredew's half were responsible for securing the engine room, while Nobby Clarke's – of which Cabby and I formed part – was to keep the enemy in the tanker's superstructure occupied. When we drew arms, a few of us, myself included, were given Lanchester sub-machine guns, but the majority were issued with rifles and bayonets. We then prepared grapnels that would bind us to the tanker once we were alongside.

We began moving into the fjord in the early hours of

the morning. The ship was completely blacked out and we proceeded at our slowest speed to avoid creating a wash that might be seen by the enemy. In the inky blackness, *Arum* herself must have been almost invisible against the dark, looming mountains on either side.

As we edged round a bend we saw the tanker, anchored in mid-fjord with her bows towards us. Lights were showing through various windows in the superstructure. In a whisper, Mr Rutherford told us to take cover behind the bulwarks. I began to feel very nervous and Cabby must have sensed my fear.

"Stick by me, Nipper," he hissed into my ear. "That Lanchester of yours is a useful item, but if there's any rough-house stuff, leave it to me."

We glided slowly towards the enemy ship. Suddenly, shouts in German reached us across the water. Seconds later, a machine gun opened fire from the tanker's bridge. Bullets smacked against our steel plating or went whining off into the distance. Our Oerlikons went into action at once, silencing the enemy gunner and raking the entire superstructure. There was the sound of shattering glass. We slid alongside with hardly a bump.

"Boarders away!" shouted the Captain from the bridge.

The grapnels went sailing over to hook on to the tanker's rail. I had forgotten how small *Arum* was, for the other ship's deck was above our level and it was quite a scramble up the ropes. I saw a white face appear at one of the bridge windows. A bullet clanged off the deck beside me. I fired a burst at the window. There was a yell and the face disappeared. Then there were running figures everywhere. I saw Nobby Clarke reach a door leading into the superstructure, toss a grenade inside and slam it shut. The explosion was followed by screams. I was dimly aware of cheering and hammering from somewhere below. Our party had taken whatever cover they could find and were firing at any likely source of resistance.

It was over very quickly. As Slim snapped on *Arum*'s searchlight to illuminate the scene, the German engine-room staff were shepherded on to the deck by Mr Merredew and some of his party. Firing ceased. Through his loudhailer, the Captain told the Germans in the superstructure that he would blow it apart piece by piece with the 4-inch gun unless they came out one by one with their hands raised. They did so, nervously, and were ordered to sit in a huddled group under guard. Next, we released the cheering British prisoners from the tank in which they had been confined. There were nearly 100 of them, officers and seamen from merchant vessels sunk by an enemy commerce raider named *Geier* in the Indian Ocean and South Atlantic, where U-boats were rarely present and some individual sailings were still permitted. They told us that at intervals *Geier*, which means "Vulture", met up with the tanker we had just captured to replenish her fuel and ammunition, and to hand over prisoners. They said that *Geier*'s Captain was a decent sort, but the tanker Captain was not. We therefore enjoyed bundling him and his crew into the tank in which he had held them. We handed over some weapons with which to guard them, and the recently released prisoners volunteered to take the tanker, whose name was *Bremen*, into Reykjavik, Iceland's principal port and capital.

"I've a good mind to ask for prize money," mused the Captain aloud as we escorted the tanker along the coast. "It would make us all a lot richer. I don't know how Their Lordships at the Admiralty would react to the suggestion, though."

It had indeed been a good night's work, especially as Mr Rutherford had found code books, marked charts and other documents in the German Captain's cabin. These eventually led to *Geier* being cornered and sunk by one of our cruisers.

For *Arum*, therefore, 1943 ended on a high note. Despite this, I was still worried about Cabby and how he was going to solve his problems. Since the brawl in the Baltic Fleet he had never been ashore in Liverpool unless ordered to do so on duty. I knew the reason why, but no one else did – and it caused a certain amount of speculation throughout the ship.

1944

Looking back, I can see now that we had turned the corner in 1943. By the start of 1944 there was a feeling among us that we were no longer in any danger of losing the War. The enemy was on the defensive everywhere and it was expected that the British, Canadian and American troops now concentrated in England would land in France soon and liberate that country from its German occupiers.

For those of us at sea, however, there was little change in our routine. The sea, in all its moods, still made constant demands on our endurance. Nor were we able to relax our concentration, knowing that a mistake could cost lives. On the other hand, we could see that our resources were growing steadily. Purpose-built escort carriers, with a full complement of aircraft, replaced the merchant carriers and accompanied most of our voyages. The proportion of merchant ships sunk while under our protection was dropping steadily, while the number of U-boats sent to the bottom remained high. The enemy launched fewer and fewer attacks in the mid-Atlantic and seemed to be concentrating their efforts on the western approaches to the United Kingdom.

Dad forwarded me a letter he had received from Admiral Emerson at Naval Intelligence. The Admiral had some interesting things to say.

Regarding the sinking of the hospital ship, I have to say that as a deliberate act this is uncharacteristic of the enemy. It is true that von Schleigen was responsible, but he claims that the torpedo was aimed at another ship and suffered a malfunction that took it off course. This happens, of course, but there is no way of verifying what he says, one way or the other.

You may have heard that in September 1942 the liner Laconia was torpedoed and sunk. She had a large number of Italian prisoners aboard, as well as women and children. The U-boat Captain responsible, a decent sort, was horrified when he discovered what he had done. He tried to save as many as possible and summoned help from wherever he could by radio. The rescue operation was going well when he was attacked by an American aircraft and forced to dive. As a result, many people were needlessly drowned.

This caused uproar in Berlin. Hitler is said to have raved that the survivors of merchant vessels should be killed without mercy. Admiral Donitz, who is responsible for U-boat operations, declined to accept this and simply issued an order to the effect that U-boats were not in future to attempt rescue operations. As you might expect, von Schleigen followed the Führer's lead. We already know that he sometimes used lifeboats for target practice. Now, he sets about the occupants with his machine guns. The trouble with massacres is that someone might survive, and that has happened in this case. Two desperately wounded men were picked up from a lifeboat by one of our destroyers and they have confirmed beyond doubt that a crowned wolf was painted on the conning tower of the U-boat responsible.

The old anger surged up inside me. It seemed so unfair that when so many U-boats had been sunk, this cold-blooded murderer had somehow managed to survive. I was certain that he had only done so by cowardly attacking targets that presented no threat to him.

On 6 June we learned that the Allies had landed in Normandy. The news was greeted with applause throughout the ship and the Captain ordered an extra issue of rum to celebrate. We all knew that, finally, the end of the War was in sight. From then until August the enemy made a last desperate effort to intercept the flow of war materials crossing the Atlantic. They succeeded in picking off one or two ships from the convoys we were escorting, but their success came at a price, for during the subsequent hunts the escort group sank two U-boats.

It was in the pre-dawn hours of a chilly September morning that Slim read a flashed signal that apparently originated from the escort commander. I was surprised when he suddenly stopped reading it out. Mr Swinson was Officer of the Watch.

"Well?" he snapped, testily.

"There's something wrong, sir," Slim replied. "I'll ask him to repeat – here, Nipper, take a look and see what you think."

The signal read: "INVESTIGATE SUSPICIOUS CONTACT EIGHT MILES DUE EAST."

"That's not the escort commander, sir," I said. "We know how his signallers work, and this isn't one of them."

"What's more, if it had been, they would have used the word SUSPECT and not SUSPICIOUS, sir," added Slim. "Saves time, you see. Someone is having us on."

Mr Swinson looked thoughtful and finally reached a decision. "Just the same, acknowledge," he said. "If you're right, let him think we've been taken in." He turned to the voice pipe. "Captain on the bridge, if you please, sir."

"Right, what's happening?" Commander Kemp asked as he arrived, rubbing the sleep out of his eyes.

Mr Swinson explained, adding that neither Slim nor I believed the signal to be genuine, although it had been sent from the same bearing as the escort commander's destroyer.

"Anything new on the scan?" the Captain shouted into the Radar office.

"No, sir," came Egghead's voice. "Yes – hang on – yes,

there is – looks like a small boat between us and the escort commander. It's moving left. Now it's gone!"

Suddenly the Asdic produced an echo.

"Contact green one-oh, extreme range, moving left, sir!" said Pingy's loudspeaker.

"Sound Action Stations!" ordered the Captain. "I know what he's up to. Remember the last trip – an escort was sent off on a wild goose chase and we lost a ship when a U-boat slipped through the gap he'd left. Well they won't catch us with the same trick."

"Contact now red oh-five still moving left, sir!" said Pingy.

The Captain ordered a change of course to port, and issued instructions for Sparks to report the contact to the escort commander.

"Contact now red one-five – seems to have changed course to due east, sir."

"Got it!" the Captain exclaimed. "He's circling round so as to pass through the hole we've just left in the escort screen. Well, before he knows it we'll be treading on his tail, and he won't like it one bit!"

We came round to port again. I swear the Captain was almost enjoying himself.

"Contact now red four-oh, sir. He's changed course again – heading back towards the convoy, I think."

The Captain gave a helm order that would place us on an

interception course. The echo on the Asdic became more and more rapid. The tension on the bridge was unbearable.

"Contact moving right, sir!" reported Pingy. "He must have picked us up on his hydrophones. Range five hundred and closing."

"Bit late in the day for him to take evasive action," mused the Captain. He leaned over the bridge rail. "Stand by with your Hedgehog, Mr Leigh – I'm going to nail this one good and proper."

"Aye aye, sir!" answered the Sub-Lieutenant.

Directed by Pingy, the Captain ordered the necessary course alterations so that we stayed on the U-boat's tail, whichever way he twisted or turned. The Asdic echoes became increasingly rapid.

"We're right behind him, sir! Seems to be going deeper."

"Hedgehog, fire! Stand by, depth charges!"

The Hedgehog bombs, set to explode at different depths in a pattern around the target, went sailing over the bows. The advantage of the system was that until they actually exploded, they did not interrupt the Asdic contact.

"Simultaneous echo, sir!" reported Pingy as we passed over the spot where the bombs had fallen.

At the Captain's order, the depth charges went rolling over our stern. Seconds later, the sea behind us erupted in fury. We could feel the ship shudder as the effect of the combined explosions reached us through the water.

"Phew! I'm glad I'm not on the receiving end of that!" commented Slim.

"Bring her round hard a'starboard!" the Captain ordered the helmsman. "Gun crews, stand by – if he surfaces it will be on our starboard side. If he doesn't we'll give him another dose of the same medicine."

As always, the sea in the target area was settling into a flat calm. Suddenly, this was broken by huge air bubbles. As the grey snout of the U-boat appeared, men began tumbling out of the conning tower and hatches. They made no attempt to man their guns and it was obvious that there was no fight left in them.

"Stop engines. Out scramble nets."

We came to a standstill just 20 yards from the stricken submarine. Led by a man in a white cap, the crew began to swim towards us. The U-boat was sinking fast, but before it disappeared beneath the waves, I saw an emblem painted on the side of the conning tower. It was faint and weathered, but unmistakably that of a crowned wolf. I gripped the rail so hard that my knuckles went white and continued to stare at the spot where the submarine had sunk.

"What's up, Nipper?" asked Slim. "You look as though you've seen a ghost!"

"Oh, it's better than that!" I said through clenched teeth. At last I was about to meet the man who had murdered my father's officers, and many other innocent seamen besides.

For most of the time my desire for revenge had remained submerged deep inside me, but now it surfaced in a boiling rage.

As the white-capped enemy commander began to climb the bridge ladder, followed by one of his officers, I saw the face I had seen many times in the papers Dad received from Admiral Emerson – the close-set eyes, the wispy ginger beard and the arrogant expression.

"My name is Kemp," said the Captain as he reached the top of the ladder.

"And mine is von Schleigen, Captain," said the German. "So, you have won our little contest. Luck was on your side, I think, or the result would have been different."

Without thinking I shoved the Captain to one side and hit von Schleigen in the mouth with every ounce of strength I possessed. He fell back down the ladder, on top of the second German officer, and the two of them ended up in a battered tangle on the deck below. I would have followed him down to continue the beating, but Slim grabbed me from behind.

"Easy, Nipper, easy now! What's got into you, lad?" he said.

"Yes, Rogers, that's what I'd like to know," snapped the Captain. "Quite apart from thumping a prisoner, there's the small matter of manhandling your commanding officer, so you'd better explain yourself and be quick about it."

"I'm sorry about that, sir, I just couldn't stop myself," I said, the anger beginning to drain out of me. "That man is a murderer. He murdered my father's officers and he'd have murdered my father if he'd had the chance. He's also murdered many other innocent merchant seamen in cold blood. I've got a file on him in my locker, including some letters from Admiral Emerson at Naval Intelligence."

"Have you, now?" said the Captain, eyeing me thoughtfully. "Always thought there was a bit of the dark horse about you. Well, you'd better go and get it, then, hadn't you?"

The prisoners had been assembled in the mess deck. Several of them grinned at me.

"We wish to thank you for hitting Kapitanleutnant von Schleigen so very hard," said one as I passed. "We have wished to do so many times because he and his officers treat us like pigs."

I told them that it had been a pleasure, then I retrieved the file from my locker and returned to the bridge. The two German officers were there, von Schleigen with blood congealing on his beard, and the other with a growing egg on his head where it had struck the deck. As soon as I appeared, von Schleigen pointed at me and began bellowing.

"That is the man who struck me! Is he an example of the discipline in your famous Royal Navy? I demand that you punish him severely at once! Also, I demand that we are treated with the respect due to German officers!"

"And I would remind you that the only person who makes demands on my bridge is me," answered the Captain coldly as he took the file from me. "Now, shut up and stand still or I'll let him loose on you again."

He read slowly through the file. Once he had absorbed its contents he handed it to me with instructions that it should be placed in the ship's safe. Then he turned to von Schleigen again, a look of cold anger in his eyes.

"Even if half this is true you are a war criminal and will end your days dangling from a hangman's rope. You are a disgrace to the German Navy and I would hang you myself if I could. There is no room for you among decent seamen aboard this ship, so I am having you and your friend confined to the paint locker. It is dirty, dark, smelly and just the place for vermin like you. Get 'em off my bridge, Chief."

Nobby Clarke almost flung the pair of them down the ladder.

"Feel better now, Rogers?" asked the Captain.

"Yes, sir, very much," I replied. "And I'm really sorry about shoving you like that."

"Maybe I'd have done the same in your position," he said, with a twinkle in his eye. "By the way, if you have any more files like that tucked away in your locker, I'd like to see them. I am supposed to run things around here, you know."

"Aye aye, sir," I said, feeling a large grin spreading across my face.

When we reached port two days later, the U-boat's crew

were marched off under a military police escort, but von Schleigen and his First Lieutenant were driven off in separate cars for interrogation. With them went the file I had put together on their crimes.

That was the last U-boat we sank, although it was not the last we saw and certainly not the last we hunted. When the Allies broke out of their Normandy beachhead the German Navy was forced to abandon all its U-boat bases in France. After this the U-boats could only operate from bases in Germany or Norway, and as this meant they had much further to go they tended to operate much closer to the British Isles. Although the net was closing they were still dangerous opponents and we could not afford to relax for one minute.

Shortly before Christmas I was promoted to Leading Seaman. I planned to buy everyone drinks in the Baltic Fleet but, once again, Cabby declined to come ashore. He had been very quiet over the past few months and seemed depressed.

"You're not worried about bumping into that crowd from London again, are you?" I asked, wanting to know what was troubling him. "We gave them such a hiding last time they won't try anything like that again."

"You're right, Nipper, they won't," he said. "But I know the way the Robsons work. They're less worried about the money than the fact that I've made fools out of 'em. They'll have lost respect, and they won't like that. They'll have a contract out on me with one of their killers, so I'll not take the risk – apart from which, I don't want you or any of the lads getting caught up in this."

I understood and accepted his decision, but I knew that he could not stay aboard for ever. After all, the War was drawing to its end and the time was approaching when *Arum* would be paid off. What would happen to him then, I wondered.

1945

Hitler had made one last desperate attempt to halt the Allies with a counter-offensive through the Ardennes in Belgium, but by the new year this campaign, later known as the Battle of the Bulge, had been defeated and the British, Canadian and American armies were preparing for their final drive into Germany.

At sea, however, life remained as it had been throughout the War. We could take nothing for granted and still had to protect our convoys with as much care as ever, for there were still U-boats about and they remained determined to sink as many of our merchant ships as possible. We only lost two ships from our convoys during those months, while our escort group accounted for three enemy submarines, although we were not directly involved in their destruction.

On 7 May, Sparks received a signal that brought him running to the bridge. Commander Kemp read it, then reached for the tannoy microphone.

"D'ye hear there! This is the Captain. I have just received word that Germany has surrendered. Adolf Hitler is believed to have committed suicide some days ago. The mainbrace will be spliced immediately! That is all."

As we enjoyed our extra rum ration we could hear cheering from every ship in the convoy as the news reached them. Some of the merchantmen hoisted every flag in their lockers to celebrate. Others turned on all their lights until reprimanded by the escort commander, who feared that some U-boats might not have received the surrender signal.

We were inbound to Liverpool and were off the coast of Northern Ireland at dawn the following day when Egghead reported an unexpected contact to port. Simultaneously, the bridge lookout reported a surfaced U-boat silhouetted again the red glow of the rising sun. Action Stations was sounded and the gun crews ran to take up their positions. A light began blinking from the U-boat's conning tower.

"U-boat signalling, sir!" I reported. "I AM ORDERED TO SURRENDER TO YOU."

As we came alongside the enemy submarine, the escort commander ordered us to put a prize crew aboard and follow the convoy into the Mersey. The prize crew consisted of Mr Merredew, myself as his signaller, and half a dozen hands, all of us armed with pistols or sub-machine guns.

"Here, you'd better take this," said Slim, handing me a folded White Ensign as I stepped into the boat. "Can't have the boys at Perch Rock opening fire on you, can we now?"

Fort Perch Rock was situated at the mouth of the Mersey

and, having had little to do for most of the War, might not be able to resist engaging a real U-boat.

"Find the way all right, can you?" hailed the Captain as we scrambled from our boat on to the submarine's casing. He still teased Mr Merredew about his early difficulties with navigation.

"Well, if we get lost I'll ask a policeman, sir," replied Mr Merredew, then turned to me, pointing at the German ensign. "I think we'll have that down and put a proper flag up, shall we, Rogers?"

I lowered the enemy's flag and handed it to him, then ran up the White Ensign. The German officers on the conning tower were expressionless, Mr Merredew sent all but the Captain below, telling them to stand down the whole crew except the engine-room staff and the helmsman. The rest of our boarding party followed them to keep an eye on things. Our convoy was already disappearing towards the horizon and, with *Arum* hurrying after it, I suddenly felt very exposed to danger.

"We'll proceed on the surface, Captain," said Mr Merredew to the U-boat commander. "I'll work out a course for you to steer – meanwhile, order full ahead, if you please."

The German gave the necessary orders into the voice pipes and the U-boat began to surge forward. There was no sound of disturbance from below and the enemy seemed willing to co-operate.

"Will you be going back to the bank when you're demobbed, sir?" I asked after a while.

"Not a chance!" he replied, laughing. "I'm going to start a boatyard on the Isle of Wight."

"I expect your father will be disappointed you're not going in with him," I said, somewhat surprised.

"Oh, he hit the roof when I told him – threatened to cut me off without a penny. I told him that after five years at sea I wasn't going to be pushed around by him or anyone else. What's more, I'd get the backing elsewhere. Couldn't believe his ears. He calmed down when he saw I meant business and now he's backing me himself. I should have stood up to him years ago."

As we entered the North Channel a Sunderland flying boat, huge and menacing, circled us suspiciously. I flashed a signal to him, explaining our situation. He then roared directly overhead, saw the White Ensign and, with a wave from the cockpit, flew off.

Having been relieved on the conning tower, I descended the vertical ladder into the submarine's hull. If I thought conditions were crowded aboard *Arum*, they were palatial in comparison to those in a U-boat. I overcame a feeling of claustrophobia and was conscious of a combined smell of cooking and packed humanity. There were too few bunks for all the crew and men were sprawled everywhere there was a level space. Some slept, others simply stared blankly at the deckhead. There was an atmosphere of relief rather than hostility.

"War finish – all go home now!" said the cook, handing me a cup of coffee.

Some hours later, we stopped at the Bar lightship to let a Mersey pilot launch come alongside. Being self-employed, the bemused pilot wanted to know who was going to pay his fee. Tongue in cheek, Mr Merredew told him to send his bill to Admiral Donitz in Berlin. It was a strange feeling, travelling up the river past the Liver Building in a U-boat. People on the ferry boats and the landing stage stared at us in disbelief, and despite our White Ensign, they were less than friendly. At length, the pilot conned us into a dock where several lorries were waiting to take the U-boat's crew away. A number of senior officers came aboard to poke about, making it clear that our presence was no longer required.

When we rejoined *Arum* in Gladstone Dock we learned that the ship's company was to be sent on a week's leave, half at a time. As usual, Cabby decided to stay aboard. To my surprise, Dad was already there when I reached home. His ship had been docked at a yard on the Clyde as her engines were in need of a major overhaul. I had already told him of von Schleigen's capture and, with grim satisfaction, he was looking forward to giving evidence when the former U-boat commander came to trial.

I was worried about Cabby. I told Dad the whole story in

confidence and asked him to help. As an honest man himself, he said he could never approve of stealing, even if it was from other thieves. I told him that because the money had been laundered into old notes, it would be impossible to trace it to its rightful owners. He thought about it for a while, then said that when Cabby was discharged he would take him on as a steward. Cabby could then jump ship at a port on the other side of the Atlantic, and after that he would be on his own. We were still at war with Japan and Dad asked whether *Arum* was likely to be sent to the Pacific. It didn't seem likely, as Japan was being battered into submission and her navy had all but ceased to exist. I suddenly realized that a period of my life was coming to an end.

Indeed, when everyone had returned from leave the Captain announced that in their wisdom, Their Lordships of the Admiralty had decided that *Arum* was no longer needed. She was to be decommissioned, laid up and paid off. Glad though we were that the War was almost over, we all felt a twinge of sadness at the thought of losing what had become our second home and family. We sailed round the south coast and finally anchored in a creek near Harwich, where we began stripping the ship. It took several weeks, at the end of which the White Ensign was hauled down and we were taken ashore.

We lined up on the quayside and Commander Kemp made a short speech thanking us for everything we had done.

He said he was leaving the Navy, and would have done so much earlier if it had not been for the War. He then walked along the ranks, shaking hands and wishing everyone luck.

"What are your plans, Rogers?" he asked when he got to me.

"I'm going to study for my Fourth Mate's ticket, sir," I replied. "I'm told I'll only have to do a short period of sea time to get it."

"Well, in twenty years you'll be captain of your own cruise liner," he said with a smile. "Then, when I come aboard as a passenger, you can tell me what to do!"

We gave him three rousing cheers as he was driven off, then clambered into the lorries that would take us to the barracks where we would await posting or discharge. I took a last look at *Arum*, lying out at anchor in the creek with other decommissioned corvettes. She looked as small as when I had first seen her, and lonely and deserted.

We had already begun to disperse when, after atomic bombs had been dropped on Hiroshima and Nagasaki, Japan finally surrendered in August. Cabby's engagement had expired during the War and he was due for early release. By slipping the clerk a few pounds, he arranged for me to be released on the same day. We were given a suit of civilian clothes and, feeling very strange in them, we travelled to Liverpool together. A few days later Dad's ship came in and Cabby set off to join her. We shook hands as he boarded the tram.

"Thanks, Nipper. I'll never forget what you've done for me," he said.

I never saw him again. The tram disappeared from view, taking with it my last link with *Arum*, the little ship that had fought in such a big war.

Epilogue

It took me a little time to get used to studying again, but as soon as life returned to normal, I joined Cunard as a cadet and obtained my Fourth Mate's ticket. I keep in touch with my old shipmates. Slim is now a Petty Officer instructor at the Signals School. Egghead is a boffin living in Cambridge. He is working to develop something called television. I have heard of it but have never seen it. He says that one day we'll be able to buy our own television sets and watch sporting events, plays and all sorts of other things while they are happening. Pingy has become a deep-sea diver specializing in underwater demolition. There is plenty of work for him to do, for even in the Mersey there are still the wrecks of ships sunk by German bombers during the Blitz. Sparks has opened a shop selling radios and gramophone records. Chalky White, the cook, is working in a hotel in Brighton. No one has heard anything about Cabby and I had no idea where he was or what he was doing.

Having appeared before a war crimes tribunal, at which Dad and his old crew gave evidence, von Schleigen was hanged. His First Lieutenant and three other members of the U-boat's crew received prison sentences.

A week or two ago I received a letter from Australia. The envelope contained a sheet of paper and a small cellophane packet. There were a couple of typed lines on the paper, but no address and no signature. They read:

NIPPER, YOU ALWAYS WERE A GOOD MATE. SELL THE ENCLOSED OR PUT IT IN A SAFE PLACE FOR A RAINY DAY. BEST OF LUCK.

I knew who it was from, for when I opened the cellophane packet it contained one of the valuable stamps I had seen in Cabby's locker.

Glossary

Anti-flash Hoods – fireproof hoods worn to protect the head and neck of naval gun crews

Astern – behind; a ship going astern is travelling backwards

Bulkheads – internal partitions within a ship's hull

Cargo Holds – the internal areas in which a merchant ship's cargo is stowed

Commerce Raider – German merchant vessel armed with guns and torpedo tubes, generally disguised to conceal her true identity

Con – to steer a ship along its course

Convoy – a number of ships sailing together, accompanied by escort vessels for their protection

CPO – Chief Petty Officer

Cruiser – medium-sized warship, usually armed with 6-inch or 8-inch guns

Destroyer – large, fast escort, most frequently armed with 4.7-inch guns, torpedo tubes and depth charges

Fleet Air Arm – the Royal Navy's own air force, usually based on aircraft carriers

Garbage Scow – a small vessel engaged on menial tasks such as collecting garbage from other warships

Grapnel – a large, multiple-hooked steel implement on the end of a throwing line, used when boarding an enemy vessel

Halyard – a rope used for raising and lowering flags

Helmsman – the seaman responsible for steering a ship by means of the helm, i.e. ship's wheel

Hull Plating – the outer skin of a ship's hull

Hydrophone – instrument for picking up under-water sounds

Line Ahead – ships following in line behind the leading vessel

List – to lean either to port or starboard

Newfoundland Escort Force – see Western Approaches Command

Port – the left-hand side of a ship, looking forward

Starboard – the right-hand side of a ship, looking forward

Troopship – either a purpose-built or converted passenger liner, used to carry a large number of soldiers

Western Approaches – those areas where sea lanes from the west converge on the British Isles

Western Approaches Command – headquarters responsible for routing convoys and coordinating counter-attacks on U-boat packs. The Newfoundland Escort Force performed a similar role in the approaches to the North American coast.

The Battle of the Atlantic was the longest campaign of the Second World War, lasting from September 1939 until the German surrender in May 1945. The German Navy's objective was to starve the United Kingdom into surrender, using not only its expanding U-boat arm but also a surface fleet and commerce raiders, while the Luftwaffe's long-range Condor squadrons attacked Allied shipping from the air. The acquisition of bases on the French and Norwegian coasts enabled the Germans to broaden the scope of their operations. Despite adopting the convoy system almost immediately, the British suffered from a lack of escorts, many of which were retained in home waters until the threat of invasion had passed. During this period the U-boats began operating in packs, attacking at night on the surface, where the escorts' Asdic was less effective.

After the threat of invasion had passed, the British response became more coordinated with the establishment of Western Approaches Command at Liverpool and the Newfoundland Escort Force at St John's. The Condor menace was reduced by the introduction of CAM ships and escort carriers, while the RAF's Coastal Command operated against U-boats off the west coast of Europe. Frustrated, the U-boats began operating off the West African coast, but following the entry of the United States into the War at the end of 1941 their efforts were concentrated in the Caribbean, the Gulf of Mexico and the east coast of the Americas, where the tonnage of Allied shipping sunk reached a peak.

Throughout 1940–1942 the German strategy appeared to be succeeding. The year 1943 also began badly for the Allies, but by this time science was beginning to work in their favour. It became possible to fix the position of a transmitting U-boat by means of High Frequency Direction Finding. Escorts fitted with the Type 271 centimetric radar could pick up objects as small as a U-boat's conning tower, making surfaced attacks at night extremely dangerous. The forward-firing Hedgehog, introduced in the spring of 1943, enabled Asdic contact to be maintained throughout an engagement. Air-to-Surface (ASV) airborne radar and Leigh Lights enabled Coastal Command to detect and destroy surfaced U-boats at night; and the arrival of the B-24 Liberator long-range bomber closed the air-cover gap that had existed in the mid-Atlantic. In addition, the number of escorts had increased appreciably, enabling the Allied navies to form hunter-killer support groups, the sole purpose of which was the destruction of U-boats. By the end of May 1943 the number of U-boats sunk had risen dramatically. By July, the total of Allied merchant ships being launched began to exceed those lost for the first time in the War.

Admiral Donitz, the German Navy's Commander-in-Chief, while forced to admit failure, declined to give up the struggle. U-boats were fitted with the Schnorkel, enabling them to run submerged while recharging their batteries, and their anti-aircraft armament was improved. Despite this, their losses continued to mount while their monthly sinkings were often trivial, only once exceeding 100,000 tons for the rest of the War. Furthermore, the German defeat in France in 1944 deprived them of their best bases. Thereafter, their activities were confined to the approaches and coastal waters of the British Isles. Latterly, U-boat crews were considered lucky if they survived three patrols. Ironically, if the campaign had continued beyond May 1945, the newest U-boats entering service were capable of much longer submerged endurance as well as being able to outrun the Allied escorts.

If the Allies had lost the Battle of the Atlantic, the British capacity to wage war would have been severely damaged, it would have been impossible to mount the D-Day invasion of Europe, and Hitler would have been free to concentrate his efforts against the Soviet Union. The cost, however, had been high. A total of 3,843 Allied merchants ships were sunk during the battle and approximately 30,000 British merchant seamen lost their lives. By far the greatest proportion of these losses were inflicted by U-boats. In comparison, the losses inflicted by German naval surface units, commerce raiders and the Luftwaffe were small. A total of 785 U-boats were sunk. Of the 39,000 officers and men who volunteered for service in U-boats, 32,000 were listed as killed or missing and 5,000 were taken prisoner. One curious fact about the battle is that both sides had broken the other's code and, except for short periods, were able to intercept and read each other's radio signals, the British through Ultra via decoded Enigma signals and the Germans through their B-Dienst interception and decoding service.

It must be said that the murderous U-boat captain in Peter's story was the exception rather than the rule, but such men did exist. Their actions reflected on the whole German submarine service, with the result that U-boat survivors were sometimes roughly handled by their captors. Many of the incidents in the story are based on real events. On Christmas Day 1940 the Flower Class corvette *Clematis* took part in a surface engagement with the German heavy cruiser *Hipper*. The re-boarding of the burning tanker *Santa Isadora* is based on the November 1940 voyage of *San Demetrio*. In February 1940, *Altmark*, supply ship to the German pocket battleship *Graf Spee*, was captured in a Norwegian fjord by the destroyer *Cossack* in circumstances very similar to *Arum*'s capture of the supply ship *Bremen*.

Peter believed that he was nicknamed Nipper because of his size and age, but this was only part of the reason, for the nickname goes far back into the days of the sailing navy. When a warship's anchor was being raised, the anchor cable was secured to a travelling rope by "nips". The rope, known as a "traveller", led the cable towards the hatch through which it was lowered into the cable tier. The "nips" were removed as they reached the hatch. The boys who did this work were known as "nippers". The nipping and un-nipping had to be done quickly, hence the term "nippy".

After the capture of *Bremen*, Commander Kemp, Peter's captain, mentions the subject of prize money. Historically, this was awarded to Royal Navy ships for the capture or sinking of enemy vessels and was an incentive for their crews to fight hard. However, in the Second World War the position was complicated not only by the fact that the Navy fought surface, submarine and, with the Fleet Air Arm, air actions, but also by the widely differing nature of the enemy vessels captured or sunk. Instead of awarding prize money to individual ships, therefore, the Admiralty decided that it would be fairer to assess a total figure for the entire war, then distribute it throughout the Navy in the form of a post-war bonus payment.

TIMELINE

4 September 1939 Passenger liner *Athenia* sunk by U-30 within hours of war being declared.

14 October 1939 Battleship HMS *Royal Oak* torpedoed and sunk in Scapa Flow by U-47 (Kapitanleutnant Gunther Prien).

May–June 1940 German Army overruns France. French harbours become available as U-boat bases.

May–October 1940 The first of the U-boats' "happy times". During this period 606 Allied merchant ships (total over 2,331,000 tons) were lost in the North Atlantic, with only nine U-boats sunk.

March 1941 Two U-boat aces, Gunther Prien and Joachim Schepke, killed in action, and a third, Otto Kretschmer, captured.

11 December 1941 Germany declares war on the United States of America.

Allied merchant shipping losses in the Atlantic during the year total 875 ships (over 3,295,000 tons). During the same period 28 U-boats were lost.

January–December 1942 The U-boats' second "happy time". 1,170 Allied merchant ships lost (6,150,340 tons). Peak of monthly sinkings reached in May with 136 ships (644,827 tons) and June with 131 ships (652,487 tons). During the same period 74 U-boats were lost.

12 September 1942 Passenger liner *Laconia*, with Italian prisoners of war and women and children aboard, is sunk by U-156, which is then attacked by American aircraft while coordinating rescue. U-boats prohibited from making future rescue attempts.

March 1943 Largest-ever battle between U-boat wolf packs and convoy escorts.

May 1943 The loss of 37 U-boats in a single month prompts Admiral Karl Donitz, Commander-in-Chief of the German Navy, to withdraw U-boats from the North Atlantic to European waters. The year marked a turning point in the battle. The Allies lost 383 merchant ships (2,170,310 tons) during the year, and 215 U-boats were sunk.

6 June 1944 D Day. Allied armies land in France. The subsequent campaign deprived the German Navy of its French submarine bases. During 1944, 117 Allied merchant ships (505,759 tons) were sunk and 203 U-boats destroyed.

April 1945 55 U-boats sunk, the highest monthly total of the War.

May 1945 Germany surrenders. During 1945 the Allies lost 91 merchant ships (366,777 tons) and 135 U-boats were sunk.